PUFFIN BOOKS

ONCE UPON A PLANET

Imagine you've gone back in time to when our ancestors lived under open skies . . . For clocks, calendars
and computers you have the sun, moon and stars.
Your kitchen tap, bathtub and washing-machine are
the sparkling waters of springs, rivers and oceans. A
tangle of green plants and tall trees gives you a
medicine cabinet and larder full of natural foods. And
if chilly winds *do* find their way through the nooks
and crannies in your deer-skin pyjamas, at least it is
clean, unpolluted air!

Nowadays, technology has changed our lives enor-
mously, but people are still part of the natural world
in a very real way. We need light and heat from the
sun to grow food, and keep our spirits up. Our bodies
are seventy per cent water, like the surface of the
planet. Our bones and muscles are formed from the
same minerals and metals that make up the Earth's
crust. And, as for air, well how long can we stay alive
if we stop breathing? The 'living skin' of the planet is
our life-support system, yet people are destroying it.

The stories and extracts in *Once Upon a Planet*
explore our relationship with the disappearing natural world and reflect its colour, power and beauty in
their writing. These tales of wit, wisdom and adventure by some favourite children's authors, past and
present, come from around the globe.

ONCE UPON A PLANET

An anthology of stories and extracts
in aid of Friends of the Earth

Selections made and introduced by
Christina Martinez

Foreword by Jonathon Porritt
Illustrated by Michael Foreman

PUFFIN BOOKS

PUFFIN BOOKS

Published by the Penguin Group
Penguin Books Ltd, 27 Wrights Lane, London W8 5TZ, England
Penguin Books USA Inc., 375 Hudson Street, New York, New York 10014, USA
Penguin Books Australia Ltd, Ringwood, Victoria, Australia
Penguin Books Canada Ltd, 10 Alcorn Avenue, Toronto, Ontario, Canada M4V 3B2
Penguin Books (NZ) Ltd, 182–190 Wairau Road, Auckland 10, New Zealand

Penguin Books Ltd, Registered Offices: Harmondsworth, Middlesex, England

First published 1989
5 7 9 10 8 6

This selection copyright © Penguin Books, 1989
Illustrations copyright © Michael Foreman, 1989
All rights reserved

The Acknowledgements on page 190 constitute an
extension of this copyright page

Printed in England by Clays Ltd, St Ives plc
Filmset in Linotron Trump Medieval

Contents

Contents

Foreword

As a child born and brought up in London, my imagination ran far and free to the remotest, wildest corners of the Earth. For lack of a magic carpet, I relied very heavily on books to transport me beyond my concrete confines and the constant throb of traffic. Books were my passports to the natural world.

And none took me further than Rudyard Kipling's *The Jungle Book*. It was almost impossible not to identify personally with Mowgli, the man-cub, as he learned the ways of Baloo, Bagheera and Shere Khan, and the other representatives of 'the Free People' in the jungle. We all know that the jungle is not really like that, and even that it's misleading to portray its creatures through the use of human characteristics. But few stories so powerfully convey the way in which *all* creatures are connected, or in which humankind should see itself as just one part of that intricately connected web of life.

Of course, we don't always have to rely on our imagination to discover the natural world. Reality often serves just as well, especially if one is lucky enough to live in the country. But even in the midst of the city, we are summoned by the same kind of living connections – in the local park, people's gardens, or even in the smallest of window-boxes!

My generation (i.e. people born before 1950!) was not brought up to appreciate the importance of that living world. Technology was the big turn-on then, and learning about the life-support systems on which we all depend was relegated to a few biology lessons or occasional nature walks. Even now, we still take so many things for granted: where the food we eat comes from; what happens to the tons of rubbish we throw away every day; the impact of our

Foreword

ordinary lives on the air we breathe and the water we drink.

That kind of ignorance and complacency partly accounts for the world being in such a mess today. By failing to respect the rest of life on Earth, we have put our own future and that of future generations in jeopardy.

Young people today have much to learn from the error of our ways. After all, what right has one generation to muck up the prospects of their children or grandchildren? Before the coming of the White Man, the North American Indians passed on this basic wisdom from one generation to the next: 'We do not inherit the world from our ancestors, we inherit it from our children.'

The authors of the stories in *Once Upon a Planet* have understood that sacred trust – as well as knowing how to write a good story!

Jonathon Porritt, Director of Friends of the Earth
October 1988

TERRY JONES

The Glass Cupboard

from *Fairy Tales*

Terry Jones wrote this fairy tale for his own
daughter, Sally. It is a story about being greedy;
about what happens to wicked bandits who
don't give as well as take. This is a very dangerous attitude when billions of people and other
creatures share one small planet . . .

THERE WAS ONCE a cupboard that was made entirely of glass so you could see right into it and right through it. Now, although this cupboard always appeared to be empty, you could always take out whatever you wanted. If you wanted a cool drink, for example, you just opened the cupboard and took one out. Or if you wanted a new pair of shoes, you could always take a pair out of the glass cupboard. Even if you wanted a bag of gold, you just opened up the glass cupboard and took out a bag of gold. The only thing you had to remember was that, whenever you took something *out* of the glass cupboard, you had to put something else back *in*, although nobody quite knew why.

Naturally such a valuable thing as the glass cupboard belonged to a rich and powerful King.

One day, the King had to go on a long journey, and while he was gone some thieves broke into the palace and stole the glass cupboard.

'Now we can have anything we want,' they said.

One of the robbers said: 'I want a large bag of gold,' and he opened the glass cupboard and took out a large bag of gold.

Then the second robber said: 'I want two large bags of gold,' and he opened the glass cupboard and took out two large bags of gold.

Then the chief of the robbers said: 'I want three of the biggest bags of gold you've ever seen!' and he opened the glass cupboard and took out three of the biggest bags of gold you've ever seen.

'Hooray!' they said. 'Now we can take out as much gold as we like!'

Well, those three robbers stayed up the whole night, taking bag after bag of gold out of the glass cupboard. But not one of them put anything back in.

In the morning, the chief of the robbers said: 'Soon we shall be the richest three men in the world. But let us go to sleep now, and we can take out more gold tonight.'

So they lay down to sleep. But the first robber could not sleep. He kept thinking: 'If I went to the glass cupboard just *once* more, I'd be even richer than I am now.' So he got up, and went to the cupboard, and took out yet another bag of gold, and then went back to bed.

And the second robber could not sleep either. He kept thinking: 'If I went to the glass cupboard and took out two more bags of gold, I'd be even richer than the others.' So he got up, and went to the cupboard, and took out two more bags of gold, and then went back to bed.

Meanwhile the chief of the robbers could not sleep either. He kept thinking: 'If I went to the glass cupboard and took out three more bags of gold, I'd be the richest of all.' So he got up, and went to the cupboard, and took out three more bags of gold, and then went back to bed.

And then the first robber said to himself: 'What am I doing, lying here sleeping, when I could be getting richer?' So he got up, and started taking more and more bags of gold out of the cupboard.

The second robber heard him and thought: 'What am I

doing, lying here sleeping, when he's getting richer than me?' So he got up and joined his companion.

And then the chief of the robbers got up too. 'I can't lie here sleeping,' he said, 'while the other two are both getting richer than me.' So he got up and soon all three were hard at it, taking more and more bags of gold out of the cupboard.

And all that day and all that night not one of them dared to stop for fear that one of his companions would get richer than him. And they carried on all the next day and all the next night. They didn't stop to rest, and they didn't stop to eat, and they didn't even stop to drink. They kept taking out those bags of gold faster and faster and more and more until, at length, they grew faint with lack of sleep and food and drink, but still they did not dare to stop.

All that week and all the next week, and all that month and all that winter, they kept at it, until the chief of the robbers could bear it no longer, and he picked up a hammer and smashed the glass cupboard into a million pieces, and they all three gave a great cry and fell down dead on top of the huge mountain of gold they had taken out of the glass cupboard.

Sometime later the King returned home, and his servants threw themselves on their knees before him, and said: 'Forgive us, Your Majesty, but three wicked robbers have stolen the glass cupboard!'

The King ordered his servants to search the length and breadth of the land. When they found what was left of the glass cupboard, and the three robbers lying dead, they filled sixty great carts with all the gold and took it back to the King. And when the King heard that the glass cupboard was smashed into a million pieces and that the three thieves were dead, he shook his head and said: 'If those thieves had always put something back into the cupboard for every bag of gold they had taken out, they would be alive to this day.' And he ordered his servants to collect all the pieces of the glass cupboard and to melt them down and make them into a globe with all the countries of the world upon it, to remind himself, and others, that the Earth is as fragile as that glass cupboard.

COLIN THIELE

Bushfire

from *February Dragon*

Forest fires destroy hundreds of thousands of
precious trees in hot countries all over the
world. Although the bushfire in this story was
probably an accident, many are started deliberately. When the trees go, so does the oxygen
they breathe out, and many creatures are left
homeless or dead. Only dust and heat remain.

This story races along like the school bus in
the Australian outback trying to escape from
the flames. Strarvy is a teacher who, like many
Australian teachers, also drives a school bus.
Lemon is his wife. Some of the people and
places mentioned have very humorous nick-
names!

I T WAS HARD TO SAY WHO saw the smoke first. Some say it was Old Barnacle Bill, others said it was Strarvy. But it didn't matter because within a minute or two the telephone switchboards at Gumbowie and Summertown were jammed with calls. The sirens wailed urgently and the men of the Emergency Fire Service dropped whatever they were doing and ran to their fire trucks. As they did so they automatically turned their eyes to the north as if they knew already what message the wind had on its breath. Everybody else did the same; shopkeepers and barmen in the town, farmers, carriers, and contractors in the country – all turned their heads to the north and stopped still for a moment. They were reading the story of the smoke.

A smudge as big as a mountain was spreading across the sky. It was the colour of dirty sulphur and growing with terrible speed. They knew what that meant. The fire was already in the Big Scrub, with a wind like a blast furnace behind it. For fifty miles it had endless food to feed on. The country was rough, with no fire-breaks and few good roads.

The men knew what was happening. From miles around they came streaming in to give help, long before the special calls went out over the radios and telephones asking for volunteers. It was going to be the bitterest fight for years.

By two o'clock the first news started to come back to Gumbowie, but it was confused. The fire was travelling so fast that even the fire-control officers with their walkie-talkie radios couldn't get a very clear picture. But everyone knew that things were bad. The whole sky was dark now, and the sun was hidden by huge loops and swirls of copper-coloured cloud. The air reeked of smoke. The fire was five miles wide, people said, and spreading quickly like an opening fan.

By half past two the reports were worse still. The wall of fire was ten miles wide and was roaring through the Big Scrub like an express train. Although ten EFS Units* and five hundred volunteers were now battling their hardest they could barely make a mark. There was talk of abandoning the Scrub and trying to burn breaks out in the open stubble. But that meant giving up twenty or thirty miles of country without a fight.

At the Upper Gumbowie school the headmaster came in to Strarvy. 'I think we'd better send the children home,' he said. 'Their parents will be getting anxious. Bus people first, and as soon as you can.'

'Yes, sir,' Strarvy said.

When the teachers dismissed their classes soon after half past two, Resin, Turps, and Columbine came tumbling out and ran for the bus at the gate.

'Gosh! Look at the smoke!'

They all stopped short. 'Jeepers!'

'I've never seen it like that before.'

'Ugh! It hurts your nose.'

'Your eyes and throat, too.'

'What about the men trying to fight it? I'll bet some of them are nearly blind.'

* EFS Units: Emergency Fire Service Units: a volunteer fire brigade.

They were right. A few of the firefighters were beginning to straggle back into Gumbowie. Their eyes were red and sore. Some of them had damp handkerchiefs tied over their mouths and noses, but they coughed and rasped just the same. Two had been overcome by the heat and suffocating smoke and had to be helped into the Community Hall where the women of the town had set up an emergency bushfire centre.

The children heard some of the men shouting to one another. 'It's past Marble Gap! Nothing'll hold it now.'

'We were in Conroy's Gully when it came thundering down the slope. Never seen anything like it. Lucky to get out alive.'

'Makes a flame-thrower look like a candle.'

The children were agog and a little afraid. More and more truckloads of men streamed through the town. Now and then a car or a fire-control officer in a jeep tore past urgently.

Strarvy came running from the school, shepherding Lemon before him and calling to the bus children to get on board.

'Hurry,' he shouted.

He counted their heads quickly as they scrambled up the steps and flopped into their seats.

'Twenty-two, twenty-three, twenty-four . . .' He looked around in exasperation. 'There's always someone missing. Who is it?'

'Burp, sir.'

'I might have known. Where is he *this* time?'

'Over at the hall, sir.'

'Whatever for?'

'Finding out about the fire I think, sir.'

Strarvy climbed into the driver's seat, blew a loud blast on the horn, and started the engine. He was just starting to move off when Burp came catapulting out of the Community Hall, shot across the street, and swung himself on board.

'Sorry, sir,' he panted, forestalling Strarvy's reprimand. 'I was just checking on the fire.'

'And what is the verdict, Captain?' Strarvy asked sarcastically.

Burp's forehead was wet with perspiration, and his freckles stood out as pink and thick as the spots on a miner's egg.

'Bad, sir. The men are retreating everywhere.' He wiped his forehead with his shirt sleeve. 'Gosh, the bus is hot, sir.'

Strarvy revved the engine and the bus lumbered off down the street. 'It won't be so bad once we get moving.'

'Even the wind's pretty hot, sir. And so full of smoke you can't breathe.'

He was right. Even after they had gone a mile or two the inside of the bus was stifling. But if they opened the windows it was worse.

When they came to the first stop, Brenda Wilson's mother was waiting for her in the car. 'I'll take Paula too,' she said. 'Mrs Fritsche rang me. We thought it best, with the fire the way it is. It's no day for them to be walking home from the bus.'

So Brenda and Paula went off with Mrs Wilson, and the bus ground on up the road. Visibility was getting worse and worse. The smoke, which until now had been streaming mainly above them, seemed to drop and blanket the land. Strarvy sat forward, peering anxiously through the windscreen, driving as fast as he dared. Bridget O'Brien's stop loomed up around the next bend, but Strarvy wouldn't open the door to let her out. He turned anxiously to Lemon.

'We can't put her down in this,' he said in a low voice. 'Before long she won't be able to see her fingers in front of her face. Her parents'll be worried stiff.'

Lemon agreed. 'I don't think we should let anyone off the bus. Not until things get better.'

'They won't get better, that's for certain. Not for a long time, anyway.'

'What shall we do, then? There's no point in taking them back to school. It's probably locked up anyway.'

Lemon looked back at the rows of hot, flushed faces behind her. 'Bring them home,' she said.

'Home?'

'To our place, Humpty Doo. We'll give them all a drink and settle them down comfortably until the danger is over. Then we can run them home afterwards.'

Strarvy looked approvingly at his new wife. 'Good idea,' he said, and drove off quickly down the Summertown road that led up past Humpty Doo, Bottlebrush Barn, Old Barnacle's store, and the wide straggling farms of the Pines, Heáslips, and Dobsons.

It was only another nine or ten miles to Humpty Doo, but Strarvy soon saw how difficult the trip was going to be. The smoke grew thicker, the heat grew worse. Twice he nearly collided with trucks racing back the way they had come.

'It's sweeping down on Gumbowie,' one of the drivers yelled. 'We'll have the fight of our lives to save the town.' Strarvy accelerated and sent the old bus lurching forward.

'At that rate it won't be long before it cuts the road behind us,' he said to Lemon, 'but what about the track ahead?' Five miles further on he suddenly had his answer. The air was now thick with ash and drifting cinders, bits of blackened leaves and burnt grass, that were swept along and shredded by the wind. The stench of smoke swirled into the bus filling the air with murk, and smarting in their eyes and throats.

Strarvy set his lips and drove on desperately. In his heart he was starting to be afraid; in his mind he was searching for advice, trying to remember a place where he and the children would be safe. All along the road on his right ran parts of the Big Scrub, sweeping up the slopes to the hilly land beyond; on the left there were trees too, but cleared paddocks every so often with fences and stubble and farmhouses as well.

They had just climbed out of the dry creek bed of the Bongabilly Soak and were straightening up on the level stretch of road a mile from Humpty Doo when some of the children yelled.

'Look! Look!'

Then there was a babble of shrieks and cries, out of which Strarvy and Lemon heard only Burp's bellowing.

'Go for your life, sir! It's the fire!'

But Strarvy had already seen it. The whole crest of the slope above them suddenly boiled over with flame, as if a crimson sea had swept the top of the ridge and was tossing and leaping down the other side in wild waves of fire. Strarvy pressed the accelerator down hard and the bus roared down the road through the dust and stinking smoke. Forty, fifty, sixty miles an hour, with Strarvy crouching at the wheel and every bolt in the bus jarring and rattling. It was as fast as the bus would go.

On the right the fire poured down the hillside like burning petrol from a tank. None of them – not even Strarvy or Lemon – had ever seen a big bushfire close at hand, and its horror stunned them. The noise was sickening, the sight unbelievable. Huge masses of flame like outbursts from the sun's rim broke away from the fire and shot high into the air, flapping and folding in fierce incandescent sheets. Whole trees exploded into torches. There was fire on the ground, and fire like hellish harpies in the air. The whole world was writhing and flinging, convulsing, twisting . . . and dying.

Up the road the bus flew, with the fire not a quarter of a mile away. Past the gates of Humpty Doo they shot, with Lemon pressing her hands to her head and crying out, 'The house! Oh, my God, what about my things!' Between the two rows of big gums on either side of the road they rocketed, with the leaves twisting in the heat and the oil in them vaporizing like benzine.

'The fallow paddock, sir!' It was Burp's voice in Strarvy's ear again. 'Turn into our gate, and head for the fallow paddock past the dam.'

Strarvy had thought of it too. The only spot in the district, an oasis of earth in a world of fire, Heaslip's ploughed paddock beckoned him on through the smoke and heat. The bus seemed as if it was about to burst into flame. Columbine and Debby had slumped in their seats; the big trees were blowing up like gunpowder behind them. But like an escaping colt with whips of fire cracking at its heels the bus swung through Heaslip's gate and tore down the track. Behind them the whole world had disappeared in smoke and flame – the Big Scrub and Humpty Doo, Barnacle's store and Bottlebrush Barn – all swallowed alike in the fiery holocaust. Almost beside them now, the fire was racing in the long stubble and grass of Heaslip's paddock. Ahead lay the chocolate handkerchief of fallow they were straining to reach. But they didn't quite make their goal. A quarter of a mile inside Heaslip's farm, where the track turned to skirt round the yabbying dam, Strarvy did what Mrs Heaslip had always been saying someone would do. A tyre, tormented by heat and angular gravel, suddenly burst with a bang. Strarvy instinctively swung the wheel, and the next moment the bus lurched off the track and headed straight for the dam. There was a flurry of wheels in mud, a squelching slide, and a final tremendous splash. Luckily the bus remained upright. There was a moment of stunned silence, then a babble of shouts and cries. Strarvy jumped quickly from the driver's seat and strode up the sloping centre aisle.

'Everyone all right?'

'Ye-e-es.'

There were a few jarred wrists and bruises, but no one was badly hurt.

'All out!' Strarvy ordered, trying to make a joke of it. 'This is the special stop for today.' The water was lapping the entrance steps, but it was only two feet deep, and one by one Strarvy and Lemon helped to shuffle the children to the shore.

'Wow!' Resin said, wading ahead and trying to cheer up poor little Columbine, who was pale and exhausted. 'What if the big blue yabby gets Burp by the toe again?'

But there wasn't much laughter about any more. The fire

had swept past them and was now far ahead, breaking across the distant stubble in a low red wave. Behind them, and all around, was a world of smoke and blackness – black for cinders, black for ashes, and black for mourning. The smoke and stench still covered everything; and dotted all over the landscape like bitter red roses on the black earth were burning things – logs and fallen trees, stumps and limbs, fence posts and farm buildings.

Some were small and idly glowing, others were fountains of fire streaming with flame in the wind. Every now and then a tree crashed down on the slope of the Big Scrub with a wild shower of sparks like a gigantic Roman candle. The air was dirty with smoke and ash, the sky hidden. And now that the monster had rushed past and devoured everything there was a strange silence, the ominous silence of desolation, like a landscape on the moon.

How long they sprawled on the bank of the dam no one knew. Perhaps they were a little light-headed from the heat, the mad race with the fire, and the crash into the dam. They were a forlorn lot on their little unscarred island in the middle of the great ring of devastation; the bus with its rump stuck up in the air and its nose under the water like a fat old pig in a bath; all the barefooted dirty-faced children lolling about listlessly like shell-shocked refugees; and Lemon, her muddy shoes and stockings in a pitiful little heap beside her, and her eyes weeping from grief and smoke, burying her head in her hands and repeating over and over, 'Our new home and all our lovely things! Our new home and all our lovely things!'

It may have been no more than an hour but it seemed a day before any other living creatures moved in that deserted land.

But at last they came – first a truck careering up the burnt-out road; then a car, and shortly afterwards three cars and a jeep. Some of them stopped at the remains of Barnacle's store, some turned up the track to Bottlebrush Barn, and some raced straight past. Straivy ran up the track towards the road, and the children stood up on the bank of the dam waving and yelling. One or two drivers saw them and swung down the track. Mr Pine was among them driving a truck, with his wife following close behind in the car. He had been fighting the fire further up the Summer-town road when the wind had suddenly swept it through his own farm; his wife had come hurrying back from the CWA meeting at Ochre Flat but had not been able to get through the line of fire till now. They both jumped from their vehicles and ran towards the children. And Resin and Turps, dragging Columbine between them, hurried forward too.

'They're safe, Harry!' they heard their mother cry. 'They're safe! They're safe!' Then she rushed up to them and grasped them, all three of them together, and held them so tightly that Columbine squeaked a protest: 'Ow, Mum, you're hurting me! You're squeezing my arm!'

'Thank God,' their mother was saying fervently, not as an answer to Columbine's squeak, but as a prayer of gratitude.

Other parents were rushing up too – Mr and Mrs Dobson, Mrs O'Brien and Mr Hammond, and even old Emil Eckert. Emil's face was as black as a minstrel's, his hair was half singed from his head, and his eyes were the colour of carrots. But nobody laughed at the way he looked. For Emil had fought with a heart like a lion; he had rescued two men from almost certain death when they had collapsed, by carrying them, one under each arm, back to the fire truck and driving them to safety. He was a hero, a VC winner in his way, but he had lost everything he owned.

'At leas' d'shildrens is safe,' he said, sagging from exhaustion. 'T'ank God for dat! One time we t'ink maybe d' fire has got dem too.'

One by one the children were picked up and driven back to Gumbowie. By a desperate effort the town had been saved, all but two or three houses on the outskirts, and now a big relief plan was being organized to give food and shelter to the refugees from the fire.

'That accounts for them all,' Strarvy said when the

last carload had been driven off. 'Now there's only the bus.'

'That'll have to wait,' Mr Pine said. 'Till someone can pull it out tomorrow.'

Mrs Pine turned to Strarvy and Lemon. 'You'd better come with us. We'll have to go to the Community Hall in Gumbowie.'

Columbine was hanging on to his mother's hand. 'Come on, Mum,' he said. 'I'm tired. Let's go home.'

Mrs Pine's eyes still seemed to be smarting from the fire. 'Columbine,' she said softly, 'don't you understand? There is no home.'

ROALD DAHL

Boy

The 'Magic Island' where Roald Dahl spent many summers as a child seems to have cast a spell on him. Here, he conjures up a blissful picture of his beautiful Norway in the years before pollution, such as acid rain, began killing its trees, lakes and wildlife . . .

THE NEXT MORNING, everyone got up early and eager to continue the journey. There was another full day's travelling to be done before we reached our final destination, most of it by boat. So after a rapid breakfast, our cavalcade left the Grand Hotel in three more taxis and headed for Oslo docks. There we went on board a small coastal steamer, and Nanny was heard to say, 'I'm sure it leaks! We shall all be food for the fishes before the day is out!' Then she would disappear below for the rest of the trip.

We loved this part of the journey. The splendid little vessel with its single tall funnel would move out into the calm waters of the fjord and proceed at a leisurely pace along the coast, stopping every hour or so at a small wooden jetty where a group of villagers and summer people would be waiting to welcome friends or to collect parcels and mail. Unless you have sailed down the Oslo-fjord like this yourself on a tranquil summer's day, you cannot imagine what it is like. It is impossible to describe the sensation of absolute peace and beauty that surrounds you. The boat weaves in and out between countless tiny islands, some with small brightly painted wooden houses on them, but many with not a house or a tree on the bare rocks. These granite rocks are so smooth that you can lie and sun yourself on them in your bathing-costume without putting a towel underneath. We would see long-legged girls and tall boys basking on the rocks of the islands. There are no sandy beaches on the fjord. The rocks go straight down to the water's edge and the water is immediately deep. As a result, Norwegian children all learn to swim when they are very young because if you can't swim it is difficult to find a place to bathe.

Sometimes when our little vessel slipped between two small islands, the channel was so narrow we could almost touch the rocks on either side. We would pass row-boats and canoes with flaxen-haired children in them, their skins browned by the sun, and we would wave to them and watch their tiny boats rocking violently in the swell that our larger ship left behind.

Late in the afternoon, we would come finally to the end of the journey, the island of Tjöme. This was where our mother always took us. Heaven knows how she found it, but to us it was the greatest place on earth. About two hundred yards from the jetty, along a narrow dusty road, stood a simple wooden hotel painted white. It was run by an elderly couple whose faces I still remember vividly, and every year they welcomed us like old friends. Everything about the hotel was extremely primitive, except the dining-room. The walls, the ceiling and the floor of our bedrooms were made of plain unvarnished pine planks. There was a washbasin and a jug of cold water in each of them. The lavatories were in a rickety wooden outhouse at the back of the hotel and each cubicle contained nothing more than a round hole cut in a piece of wood. You sat on the hole and what you did there dropped into a pit ten feet below. If you looked down the hole, you would often see rats scurrying about in the gloom. All this we took for granted.

Breakfast was the best meal of the day in our hotel, and it was all laid out on a huge table in the middle of the dining-room from which you helped yourself. There were maybe fifty different dishes to choose from on that table. There were large jugs of milk, which all Norwegian children drink at every meal. There were plates of cold beef, veal, ham and pork. There was cold boiled mackerel submerged in aspic. There were spiced and pickled herring fillets, sardines, smoked eels and cod's roe. There was a large bowl piled high with hot boiled eggs. There were cold omelettes with chopped ham in them, and cold chicken and hot coffee for the grown-ups, and hot crisp rolls baked in the hotel kitchen, which we ate with butter and cranberry jam. There were stewed apricots and five or six different cheeses including of course the ever-present gjetost, that tall brown rather sweet Norwegian goat's cheese which you find on just about every table in the land.

After breakfast, we collected our bathing things and the whole party, all ten of us, would pile into our boat.

Everyone has some sort of a boat in Norway. Nobody sits around in front of the hotel. Nor does anyone sit on the beach because there aren't any beaches to sit on. In the early days, we had only a row-boat, but a very fine one it was. It carried all of us easily, with places for two rowers. My mother took one pair of oars and my fairly ancient half-brother took the other, and off we would go.

My mother and the half-brother (he was somewhere around eighteen then) were expert rowers. They kept in perfect time and the oars went *click-click, click-click* in their wooden rowlocks, and the rowers never paused once during the long forty-minute journey. The rest of us sat in the boat trailing our fingers in the clear water and looking for jellyfish. We skimmed across the sound and went whizzing through narrow channels with rocky islands on either side, heading as always for a very secret tiny patch of sand on a distant island that only we knew about. In the early days we needed a place like this where we could paddle and play about because my youngest sister was only one, the next sister was three and I was four. The rocks and the deep water were no good to us.

Every day, for several summers, that tiny secret sand-patch on that tiny secret island was our regular destination. We would stay there for three or four hours, messing about in the water and in the rockpools and getting extraordinarily sunburnt.

In later years, when we were all a little older and could swim, the daily routine became different. By then, my mother had acquired a motor-boat, a small and not very seaworthy white wooden vessel which sat far too low in the water and was powered by an unreliable one-cylinder engine. The fairly ancient half-brother was the only one who could make the engine go at all. It was extremely difficult to start, and he always had to unscrew the sparking-plug and pour petrol into the cylinder. Then he swung a flywheel round and round, and with a bit of luck, after a lot of coughing and spluttering, the thing would finally get going.

When we first acquired the motor-boat, my youngest sister was four and I was seven, and by then all of us had learnt to swim. The exciting new boat made it possible for us to go much farther afield, and every day we would travel far out into the fjord, hunting for a different island. There were hundreds of them to choose from. Some were very small, no more than thirty yards long. Others were quite large, maybe half a mile in length. It was wonderful to have such a choice of places, and it was terrific fun to explore each island before we went swimming off the rocks. There were the wooden skeletons of shipwrecked boats on those islands, and big white bones (were they human bones?), and wild raspberries, and mussels clinging to the rocks, and some of the islands had shaggy long-haired goats on them, and even sheep.

Now and again, when we were out in the open water beyond the chain of islands, the sea became very rough, and that was when my mother enjoyed herself most. Nobody, not even the tiny children, bothered with lifebelts in those days. We would cling to the sides of our funny little white motor-boat, driving through mountainous white-capped waves and getting drenched to the skin, while my mother calmly handled the tiller. There were times, I promise you, when the waves were so high that as we slid down into a trough the whole world disappeared from sight. Then up and up the little boat would climb, standing almost vertically on its tail, until we reached the crest of the next wave, and then it was like being on top of a foaming mountain. It requires great skill to handle a small boat in seas like these. The thing can easily capsize or be swamped if the bows do not meet the great combing breakers at just the right angle. But my mother knew exactly how to do it, and we were never afraid. We loved every minute of it, all of us except for our long-suffering Nanny, who would bury her face in her hands and call aloud upon the Lord to save her soul.

In the early evenings we nearly always went out fishing. We collected mussels from the rocks for bait, then we got into either the row-boat or the motor-boat and pushed off to drop anchor later in some likely spot. The water was very deep and often we had to let out two hundred feet of line before we touched bottom. We would sit silent and tense, waiting for a bite, and it always amazed me how even a little nibble at the end of that long line would be transmitted to one's fingers. 'A bite!' someone would shout, jerking the line. 'I've got him! It's a big one! It's a whopper!' And then came the thrill of hauling in the line hand over hand and peering over the side into the clear water to see how big the fish really was as he neared the surface. Cod, whiting, haddock and mackerel, we caught them all and bore them back triumphantly to the hotel kitchen where the cheery fat woman who did the cooking promised to get them ready for our supper.

I tell you, my friends, those were the days.

HE LIYI

The Tibetan Envoy

from *The Spring of the Butterflies*

This traditional Chinese folk-tale praises two very special types of treasure.

The first is more valuable than silks and jewels: it is the wisdom and experience that the Tibetan envoy uses to try to win the hand of the Chinese princess.

The second is more precious than silver and gold: it is the seed and grain that the Tibetan prince knows will make his land green and fertile . . .

MANY YEARS AGO, THE emperor of the Tang dynasty had a most beloved daughter, the Princess Wencheng. When she was old enough to get married, all the neighbouring princes sent an envoy to the capital to propose. And the prince of faraway Tibet also sent an envoy: the wisest man in Tibet, and the most cunning.

There were seven envoys in all. All of them had the same aim, to win Princess Wencheng's love, but all were in doubt. Who would succeed? Nobody knew.

The emperor thought Tibet was too far away. It would be hard to visit his daughter there. He had no mind to let his daughter marry a Tibetan prince, though he could not refuse the Tibetan envoy openly. He held a meeting of his ministers, to consider how to reject the Tibetan prince's suit. They decided to set a hard marriage test. When the Tibetan envoy failed, perhaps he would go away and leave them to choose the princess a husband from among the neighbouring princes.

The Tibetan Envoy

On the following day, five hundred mares and their foals were brought to the city square. The foals were driven into the centre of the square, and their mothers were tied up round the edge. Then the king declared, 'All seven of the princes are as dear and useful to me as my hands and arms. I really wish I had seven princesses for them. Too bad. I have only one daughter. I don't know whom I should choose. So to be fair, I've brought five hundred mares and their foals here. Now you seven envoys, get busy matching up mothers and young. Then I'll consider the marriage.'

The seven envoys began. The six local ones rushed about, each trying to lead the foals to the mares, but the Tibetan envoy just waited politely for them to finish. Every time the envoys led a foal to the mares, all the horses bucked and kicked and made a tremendous commotion. The foals were afraid to go near. None of the envoys could match up mare and foal.

At last the Tibetan envoy's turn came. The Tibetans are very experienced with horses; they know just about everything about them. So he didn't blunder around like the others. Instead he asked for food of the best quality to be brought to the mares. All the mares stopped kicking and ate peacefully till they couldn't eat any more. As soon as they were finished, they looked up and neighed loudly. That was a call for the foals to suckle. And the foals all ran to their own mother, all sucking, prancing, licking, or happily whisking their tails.

The emperor appreciated this envoy's quick wits very much, but he still didn't want him to win. So he announced another test. 'This envoy is really very clever, and I like him too, but that's not the end. I want to give you all another chance.' He took out a piece of elegant green jade and said to the seven envoys: 'This jade is as intricate as it is beautiful. Look carefully at it, and you will find a hole twisting and turning right through it. When one of you hangs this jade on a thread, I will consider the marriage.'

The Tibetan envoy let the other six try first, but they all failed hopelessly. They tried all day but none of them could get the thread through. At last the Tibetan envoy was asked to try.

The Tibetan envoy caught an ant and tied the thread to its leg. Then he smeared a little honey on the exit hole of the jade. The ant smelled the honey, and very quickly got through the hole with the thread trailing behind. The Tibetan envoy tied the two ends together and passed the jade necklace to the king.

The emperor was very surprised. He had to think of a new test the Tibetan might fail. He said, 'We will try another competition, so that each one of you will believe I take you seriously.' Then he instructed a carpenter to take a log, and plane and polish the wood till each end looked identical. The log was shown to the envoys, and the king said, 'Here is a log. Come and examine it. I want you to make out which end comes from the top of the tree, and which from the bottom. I don't want guesswork. If any of you can explain it correctly, the question of my daughter's marriage will be easily decided.'

The six local envoys examined it first. One by one they stared at it, turned it, touched it, measured it, but none could make out which end was which. Finally they asked the Tibetan envoy's opinion.

The Tibetan envoy came from the mountains, so he knew that a tree is heavier nearer the root. He asked them to put the log into the river. It floated with the lighter end ahead, the heavier behind. He easily pointed out which was which.

The emperor was impressed by this clever solution, but he still did not want to send his daughter so far away. Therefore he called another meeting of his ministers. One of them suggested, 'Your Majesty should choose three hundred beautiful girls and dress them in the same clothes as the princess. Stand them in a line. If this envoy can tell her apart from the others, it must be fate. I don't think he can do that. In this way your daughter will remain near you.'

The emperor agreed to this, and declared, 'To be fair to all the envoys, we must have one last test. I have three hundred girls, all dressed alike. The princess is among them. He who identifies her correctly wins her for his master.'

Again the six local envoys tried first. They thought the most beautiful girl ought to be the princess, but she wasn't. All pointed out the wrong girl.

Meanwhile the Tibetan envoy was busy around the palace trying to learn about the princess. He had never seen her or heard anything specific about her. He had many friends in the palace. He visited the cart drivers, the serving men, the washerwomen, hoping to find out about the emperor's daughter. At last he met an aged laundress who knew about the girl, but told him, 'I am afraid to tell you anything. Our king has a private magician who knows all secrets. He would find me out and I should die.'

The Tibetan calmed her fears. 'Madam, you may rely on me. Tell me all you know about her. Do as I say and no magician can find you out.' Then he brought three white stones and placed them on the ground. Above these stones he fixed a large iron cauldron filled with water. Then he laid a bench across the cauldron, and sat the old woman on the bench. He gave her a brass trumpet and said, 'Speak boldly through this. The wisest magician can only say, "the speaker lives on a wooden mountain. This wooden mountain is on an iron sea. The sea is at the top of three white mountains. The speaker has a brass mouth." The emperor can never find you. He will think that "brass-mouth" must be a witch or a spirit. So, be brave and please tell me all the details you know.'

The old woman chuckled at that. She told him without the least fear, 'My gentleman, in the first place you must not point at the most beautiful girl. The princess isn't ugly but she is not the most beautiful one. She is a princess, so people usually say she is the nicest girl in the world. Second, don't point at the front row or the back row. That's too obvious. The king puts his daughter in the middle. Third, the princess has worn oil on her hair since she was a child. Bees like it, and often fly above her head. She likes

35

the bees, and never waves them away. The other girls have no oil, for the princess gets it from abroad. So if you see bees around her head, you may point at her and she will be just the right princess. That's the gossip among the courtiers. The cooks heard it from them. I washed the cooks' clothes, so I heard it from them. Now, my gentleman, that is all I can tell you. Good luck!'

The Tibetan envoy thanked her and went to make his choice. He was very careful. He didn't point at the back row or the front row, nor at the most beautiful girl. He studied the girls one at a time. At noon, he saw a golden bee dancing above a girl's head. The girl didn't mind the bee. She wasn't afraid of it, but watched it lovingly. The Tibetan envoy pointed straight at her and said, 'This is the princess.' And it was exactly just the real princess. The emperor and the other six envoys were amazed at his success.

The emperor thought: this Tibetan envoy had never seen the princess, so how did he know so much more about her than the other envoys? Somebody must have talked to him.

The emperor ordered his magician to find out the culprit. But the magician just talked a lot of nonsense.

The emperor could not help it. He had to say 'yes', and allow the Tibetan envoy to talk to the princess face to face.

The Tibetan said to her, 'Princess, I am very glad to know your father the emperor has promised to let our Tibetan prince marry the best princess on earth. As you are going away with me, the emperor will want to give you a lot of presents. Our Tibetan prince has everything you need. So don't take jewels and silks, but remember what I'm telling you now. Ask him for seeds of all the chief grains. With them we shall make our land fruitful, which is a gift more precious than gold and silver.'

The princess took his advice. Amazed at his daughter's request, the emperor gave her five hundred horses loaded with grain seeds to take with her to Tibet.

SCOTT O'DELL

Island of the Blue Dolphins

Aleut hunters come from the sea with strange weapons and empty promises. When they sail once more, the people of the Island of the Blue Dolphins have been betrayed. Their menfolk lie dead; their village is haunted by the memories of happier times, and so they abandon their island home.

Only twelve-year-old Karana will not leave. She stays to save her little brother, Ramo. But soon she is left completely alone. She tells of how, with the skill and patience of her tribe, she survives many stormy winters and further visits from the Aleut hunters; of how her companions come to be the birds Tainor and Lurai, and the wild dog Rontu. Karana also tells of her short, secret friendship with an Aleut girl, Tutok.

What shines through most in this true story that took place off the Pacific coast of North America is the courage and compassion that help Karana to survive. Here, she talks of how she values her animal family and learns to respect their lives . . .

THE HUNTERS LEFT MANY wounded otter behind them. Some floated in and died on the shore and others I killed with my spear since they were suffering and could not live. But I found a young otter that was not badly hurt.

It lay in a bed of bull kelp and I would have paddled by if Rontu had not barked. A strand of kelp was wound around its body and I thought it was sleeping, for often before they go to sleep they anchor themselves in this way to keep from drifting off. Then I saw there was a deep gash across its back.

The otter did not try to swim away as I drew near and reached over the side of the canoe. They have large eyes, especially when they are young, but this one's were so large from fear and pain that I could see my reflection in them. I cut the kelp that held it and took it to a tide pool behind the reef, which was sheltered from the waves.

The day was calm after the storm and I caught two fish along the reef. I was careful to keep them alive, because otter will not eat anything that is dead, and left them in the pool. This was early in the morning.

That afternoon I went back to the pool. The fish had disappeared and the young otter was asleep, floating on its back. I did not try to treat its wound with herbs because salt water heals and the herbs would have washed off anyway.

I brought two fish every day and left them in the pool. The otter would not eat while I was watching. Then I brought four fish and these also disappeared and finally six, which seemed to be the right number. I brought them whether the day was calm or stormy.

The otter grew and its wound began to heal, but still it stayed in the pool, and now when I came it would be waiting for me and would take the fish from my hand. The pool was not big and it could easily have got out and away into the sea, yet it stayed there and slept or waited for me to come with food.

The young otter now was the length of my arm and very glossy. It had a long nose that came to a point and many whiskers on each side and the largest eyes I have ever seen. They would watch me all the time I was at the pool, following me whatever I did, and when I said something, they would move around in a very funny way. In a way, too, that made pain come to my throat because they were gay and sad also.

For a long time I called it Otter as I had called Rontu, Dog. Then I decided to give the otter a name. The name was Mon-a-nee, which means Little Boy with Large Eyes.

It was a hard task catching fish every day, especially if the wind was blowing and the waves were high. Once when I could catch only two and dropped them into the pool, Mon-a-nee ate them quickly and waited for more. When he found that was all I had he swam around in circles, looking at me reproachfully.

The waves were so high the next day that I could not fish on the reef even at low tide, and since I had nothing to give him I did not go to the pool.

It was three days before I could catch fish and when I went there again the pool was deserted. I knew that he would leave some day, but I felt bad that he had gone back to the sea and that I would never catch fish for him again. Nor would I know him if I saw him again in the kelp, for now that he had grown and his wound had healed, he looked like all the others.

Soon after the Aleuts had left I moved back to the headland.

Nothing had been harmed except the fence, which I mended, and in a few days the house was the same as before. The only thing that worried me was that all the abalones I had gathered in the summer were gone. I would need to live from day to day on what I could catch, trying to get enough on the days when I could fish to last through the times when I could not. Through the first part of the winter, before Mon-a-nee swam away, this was sometimes hard to do. Afterwards it was not so hard and Rontu and I always had enough to eat.

While the Aleuts were on the island, I had no chance to catch little smelts and dry them, so the nights that winter were dark and I went to bed early and worked only during the day. But still I made another string for my fishing spear, many hooks of abalone shell, and last of all ear-rings to match the necklace Tutok had given me.

These took a long time, for I searched the beach many mornings when the tide was out before I found two pebbles of the same colour as the stones in the necklace and soft enough to cut. The holes in the ear-rings took even more time, for the stones were hard to hold, but when I was done and had rubbed them bright in fine sand and water, and fastened them with bone hooks to fit my ears, they were very pretty.

On sunny days I would wear them with my cormorant dress and the necklace, and walk along the cliff with Rontu.

I often thought of Tutok, but on these days especially I would look off into the north and wish that she were here to see me. I could hear her talking in her strange language and I would make up things to say to her and things for her to say to me.

Spring again was a time of flowers and water ran in the ravines and flowed down to the sea. Many birds came back to the island.

Tainor and Lurai built a nest in the tree where they were born. They built it of dry seaweed and leaves and also with hairs off Rontu's back. Whenever he was in the yard while it was being made, they would swoop down if he were not looking and snatch a beakful of fur and fly away. This he did not like and he finally hid from them until the nest was finished.

I had been right in giving a girl's name to Lurai, for she laid speckled eggs and, with some help from her mate, hatched two ugly fledglings which soon became beautiful. I made up names for them and clipped their wings and before long they were as tame as their parents.

I also found a young gull that had fallen from its nest to the beach below. Gulls make their nests high on the cliffs, in hollow places on the rocks. These places are usually small and often I had watched a young one teetering on the edge of the nest and wondered why it did not fall. They seldom did.

This one, which was white with a yellow beak, was not badly hurt, but he had a broken leg. I took him back to the house and bound the bones together with two small sticks and sinew. For a while he did not try to walk. Then, because he was not old enough to fly, he began to hobble around the yard.

With the young birds and the old ones, the white gull and Rontu, who was always trotting at my heels, the yard seemed a happy place. If only I had not remembered Tutok. If only I had not wondered about my sister Ulape, where she was, and if the marks she had drawn upon her cheeks had proved magical. If they had, she was now married to Kimki and was the mother of many children. She would have smiled to see all of mine, which were so different from the ones I always wished to have.

Early that spring I started to gather abalones and I gathered many, taking them to the headland to dry. I wanted to have a good supply ready if the Aleuts came again.

One day when I was on the reef filling my canoe, I saw a herd of otter in the kelp near by. They were chasing each other, putting their heads through the kelp and then going under and coming up again in a different place. It was like a game we used to play in the brush when there were children on the island. I looked for Mon-a-nee, but each of them was like the other.

I filled my canoe with abalones and paddled towards shore, one of the otter following me. As I stopped he dived and came up in front of me. He was far away, yet even then I knew who it was. I never thought that I would be able to tell him from the others, but I was so sure it was Mon-a-nee that I held up one of the fish I had caught.

Otter swim very fast and before I could take a breath, he had snatched it from my hand.

For two moons I did not see him and then one morning while I was fishing he came suddenly out of the kelp. Behind him were two baby otter. They were about the size of puppies and they moved along so slowly that from time to time Mon-a-nee had to urge them on. Sea otter cannot swim when they are first born, and have to hold on to their mother. Little by little she teaches her babies by brushing them away with her flippers, then swimming around them in circles until they learn to follow.

Mon-a-nee came close to the reef and I threw a fish into the water. He did not snatch it as he usually did, but waited to see what the young otter would do. When they seemed more interested in me than in food, and the fish started to swim away, he seized it with his sharp teeth and tossed it in front of them.

I threw another fish into the water for Mon-a-nee, but he did the same things as before. Still the babies would not take the food, and at last, tired of playing with it, swam over and began to nuzzle him.

Only then did I know that Mon-a-nee was their mother. Otter mate for life and if the mother dies the father will often raise the babies as best he can. This is what I thought had happened to Mon-a-nee.

I looked down at the little family swimming beside the reef. 'Mon-a-nee,' I said, 'I am going to give you a new name. It is Won-a-nee, which fits you because it means Girl with the Large Eyes.'

The young otter grew fast and soon were taking fish from my hand, but Won-a-nee liked abalones better. She would let the abalone I tossed to her sink to the bottom and then dive and come up holding it against her body, with a rock held in her mouth. Then she would float on her back and put the abalone on her breast and strike it again and again with the rock until the shell was broken.

She taught her young to do this and sometimes I sat on the reef all the morning and watched the three of them pounding the hard shells against their breasts. If all otters did not eat abalones this way I would have thought it was a game played by Won-a-nee just to please me. But they all did and I always wondered about it, and I wonder to this time.

After that summer, after being friends with Won-a-nee and her young, I never killed another otter. I had an otter cape for my shoulders, which I used until it wore out, but never again did I make a new one. Nor did I ever kill another cormorant for its beautiful feathers, though they have long, thin necks and make ugly sounds when they talk to each other. Nor did I kill seals for their sinews, using instead kelp to bind the things that needed it. Nor did I kill another wild dog, nor did I try to spear another sea elephant.

Ulape would have laughed at me, and others would have laughed, too – my father most of all. Yet this is the way I felt about the animals who had become my friends and those who were not, but in time could be. If Ulape and my father had come back and laughed, and all the others had come back and laughed, still I would have felt the same way, for

43

animals and birds are like people, too, though they do not talk the same or do the same things. Without them the Earth would be an unhappy place.

PHILIPPA PEARCE

The Nest-Egg

Philippa Pearce has written this story specially
for *Once Upon a Planet*. She says: 'My own
hens live with their cockerel in just such a little
house as in the story. They have to be shut up
every night against foxes and mink. Otherwise
they roam freely in the surrounding meadow-
land, picking and pecking.

So the hens are real hens; but William – the
human hero – is an invented character. A crisis
in his life brings humans and hens suddenly
and surprisingly close . . .'

SCHOOL WAS DREARY FOR William Penney. He was no good there. He was no good at lessons, or at games, and he was no good at making new friends. Teachers, privately warned to make allowances for him, found him difficult in a dull way. His worst stroke of luck turned out to be his name. Nothing wrong with William, you might think; but another – and better-liked – boy in the class had the same name. Everybody said he had first claim to it, since William Penney was the newcomer. So what was William Penney to be called?

Someone, with a snigger, suggested Willy; and then everybody sniggered. William did not mind much: as long as they left him alone, he could bear sniggerings.

But then someone said: 'Well, he's got a second name, hasn't he? W. H. Penney – he wrote his name once like that, I saw it. Come on, Willy! If you don't want to be called Willy, what does H stand for?'

'I don't mind being called Willy,' said William

'What does H stand for?'

'It's just my father's name.'

'Well, what *is* your father's name?'

He didn't want to tell them. He didn't want them to know his father's name, because his father was all he had now, and even he was away somewhere. His mother had died.

'I'd rather be called Willy, please.'

But now they knew he did not want to tell them, they tormented him. 'Come on, what is it? Is it Hugh? Or Hubert? Or Herbert?'

'Or Halibut!' suggested a wit; and the same boy went on: 'Or is it Halgernon? Or Hebenezer?'

So, after all, he was trapped by his own anger into telling them. Stammering in anger and haste, he cried: 'It's not a stupid name – it's not! It's just Hen – Hen –'

Then they shouted with joyous laughter and called him Hen – Hen – Henny-penny, and clucked at him and asked him what he had had for breakfast, and before he had time to answer, answered for him: 'A hegg!'

If they had only known, their teasing came near the truth. William Henry Penney really did have an egg for breakfast, whether he liked it or not, nearly every day of the week, because now he was living with his Aunt Rosa, who kept hens. She ran her garden – almost as big as a small-holding – as a business. She grew all the usual outdoor vegetables, and had a greenhouse for cucumbers and early tomatoes. At the bottom of the garden and in the orchard, she kept hens; not very many, but good layers. William helped with the hens, feeding them in the morning before he went to school, filling their drinking-bowl with fresh water, and letting them out of their run to roam in his aunt's orchard. He also collected the eggs in the evening, but this was only under Aunt Rosa's supervision. He had once broken an egg.

Until now Aunt Rosa had lived by herself, with her dog, Bessy. Aunt Rosa was middle-aged and sharp; Bessy was old and cantankerous. Neither of them was used to having children about the place.

When William's father had brought him here, he explained to his son that this was only until he could find another job in another place, and a new home for them both. 'Until then Rosa has said she'll put up with you – I mean, put you up. Very kind of Rosa,' said William's father. He did not usually think his sister was particularly kind.

'Why's she wearing that scarf of Mum's?' asked William.

His father frowned. He said: 'She's being very helpful in a bad time, and she asked if she could have it. It was one of the things she wanted.'

'I don't like her having things,' said William.

'Oh, come on, William!' his father said angrily. But William was not deceived: really, his father was angry with Aunt Rosa for wanting things that had so recently belonged to her dead sister-in-law, his own wife, William's mother. He was also angry with himself for having to give in to her.

William's father saw William settled in Aunt Rosa's house. Then he said goodbye, leaving William with Aunt Rosa and Bessy.

In Aunt Rosa's house William had a bedroom to himself, but it was big and bare and lonely after his own old room crammed with his ancient toys and his collections and gadgets and oddments, all in a friendly muddle. He could not feel at home here, in Aunt Rosa's house. Deliberately, he did not unpack his suitcase into the drawers left empty for him.

Nowadays William was always watched: he knew that. In Aunt Rosa's house he was watched by Aunt Rosa and by Bessy, in case he did anything silly, wasteful, or damaging. At school he was watched by those whose fun it was to tease him. His only really safe and private time was in bed, at night. Every night he cried himself to sleep – but quietly, so that Aunt Rosa should not hear him and despise him for crying. He had sad dreams that woke him to real sadness. Then he cried for his father, who was far away, and for his mother, who was dead.

One day, in the early evening, Aunt Rosa came down from her bedroom dressed with unusual care. Besides her good clothes, she was wearing a thin gold chain: William recognized it at once. He had saved up to buy it for his mother on her last birthday.

He couldn't help himself; he said, 'That's my mum's gold chain.'

'Yes,' said his aunt. 'It was hers. It's not real gold, of course. I wouldn't have taken anything valuable from your father, when he pressed me to choose, after the funeral. The chain's not worth anything – just rubbish. But it does for the odd occasion.'

William said nothing aloud, but to himself he said: 'I hate Aunt Rosa. I hate having to live in her house.'

His aunt was dressed up to attend a parish-meeting. Before she left, she said to William: 'You should be able to help more on your own by now. Go down to the hen-house and see if there are any eggs. Probably not; the hens are all going off lay. But, if there is an egg, for goodness' sake don't break it! And don't bring out the nest-egg, as you did last time!' The nest-egg was only an imitation egg: it was left in a nest to encourage the hen to lay other eggs there and nowhere else.

Aunt Rosa went off on her bicycle; Bessy settled herself in her basket in the kitchen; and William went down the garden to the hen-house.

He was still thinking of his mother's gold chain. Of course, he had known that it wasn't made of real gold; but his mother had loved to wear it. He remembered buying it, and keeping it a secret until her birthday. In secret he had played with it, and he could still remember the way the thin links had poured and poured between his fingers. He remembered the way his mother had looked when she wore it; and now he hated to remember how it had looked round the neck of his Aunt Rosa.

Still thinking of the gold chain, he reached the hen-house.

The hen-house was a low, wooden, home-made affair, very simple and rather ramshackle. It had a door at the back, through which the egg-collector could reach in. At the front was a pop-hole through which the hens and the cockerel went out into the run. The run had high, chicken-wire walls and a chicken-wire door that led into the orchard. The door was open, as usual in the summer day-time: William had already seen the cockerel and his hens pecking about in the grass of the orchard.

He unlatched the hen-house door and peered in. It was always dim inside the hen-house, but there was not much to see, anyway. Just an earth floor with straw over it, in which the hens hollowed their nests; a perch across from side to side, for the fowls to roost on at night; and the daylight coming in through the pop-hole on the opposite side of the hen-house.

For the first time, William was here without Aunt Rosa nagging him to hurry. He let his eyes accustom themselves to the twilight of the hen-house; and then he saw the eye watching him. It belonged to the one hen that, after all, had not gone out with the others into the orchard. She was crouching in a corner of the hen-house, deep in the straw, absolutely still, absolutely quiet, staring at him.

The hen-house was not large, but it was quite big enough for a boy of William's size to creep inside. He did so now, for the convenience of looking more thoroughly for any eggs. But he kept away from the hen sitting in her corner.

The hen-house smelled of hens – there was a line of hen-droppings in the straw under the perch: the straw would need changing soon. There was also the smell, brought out by the summer heat, of creosote in the wood. All the same, William rather liked being in the hen-house. It was a real house, in its way, and it was just his size. It fitted him; he felt at home in it.

Being careful where he put his feet down in the straw, he searched for eggs. But, as his aunt had prophesied, there was none.

His search brought him to the sitting hen. Surely she must be sitting on something? As he had seen his aunt do, he slid his hand underneath her body to feel for any eggs; but at once she began to fluster and flounder and squawk.

Her cries were immediately heard and answered from the orchard by the cockerel, who came running at a great pace and so appeared within seconds at the pop-hole, confronting William with furious enmity.

Once, recently, Aunt Rosa had remarked in scorn that William couldn't possibly be afraid of an ordinary *cockerel*; but Aunt Rosa was ignorant of a great many of life's possibilities. In this present emergency, William withdrew from the hen-house very quickly indeed, latching the door shut behind him. He heard the cockerel and the hen conferring crossly inside.

Meanwhile, William had an egg in his hand – the only egg that had been under the hen. He opened his hand, and – it was the nest-egg, after all! A good thing that Aunt Rosa was not with him! By himself, he had time to look at the nest-egg properly. It was made of earthenware, almost as smooth-surfaced as a real egg, and the same size and weight as a real egg. There were differences: the stamp of the maker's name made an unevenness of surface in one place; and there was an air-hole in the side, about the size of a hole down a drinking-straw. And the nest-egg was hollow.

William handled the nest-egg. He liked it, as he had liked being inside the hen-house. He liked the innocent trickery of it; he liked the neat little hole in its side that was also the entry to its hollow interior. And, as he studied the nest-egg, an idea began to grow in his mind . . .

He pocketed the nest-egg and went back indoors. The kitchen-door was open and Bessy watched him suspiciously from her basket, but she could see nothing wrong. He went upstairs and into his bedroom, and shut the door. He took the nest-egg from his pocket and hid it at the bottom of his suitcase.

He was in bed, waiting for sleep, when his aunt came back from her meeting. He heard her lock up, see to Bessy, and then come upstairs to her bedroom. Bessy came with her, because she slept at the foot of her bed at night. Aunt Rosa, with Bessy, went into the bedroom, and the door was shut behind them.

Now Aunt Rosa would be getting ready for bed. She would take her best coat off and hang it in the wardrobe. She would take her shoes off. She would take her dress off – but no! Before she did that, she would take off William's gold chain. She took it off and – well, where did she put it? Had she a jewel-box for necklaces and brooches? Or did she put them into some special drawer? Or did she leave them on top of her dressing-table, at least for the time being?

Worrying at uncertainties, William fell into an uneasy sleep. He dreamed sad dreams, as usual; and the saddest – and the silliest, too – was that the nest-egg had grown little chicken legs and climbed out of his suitcase and was running to catch his mother's gold chain to eat it, as though it were a worm. But the nest-egg never caught up with the gold chain.

The next morning William was woken by his aunt's calling from downstairs: his breakfast was ready. He dressed quickly and then went straight from his bedroom to his aunt's room. Her door was open, and even from the doorway he could see that his mother's gold chain lay coiled on the top of his aunt's dressing-table.

Oh! He was in luck! He had only to cross the bedroom floor and pick up the chain, and it would be his.

He took one step inside the bedroom doorway, and – he was out of luck, after all. He had forgotten that Bessy slept in his aunt's room every night; and here she still was. She lay at the foot of the bed, watching him; and, as he made that quick, furtive movement to enter the bedroom, Bessy growled. He knew that if he went any further, she would begin to bark – to shout to Aunt Rosa the alarm: 'Thief! Thief!'

He was bitterly disappointed, but he had no choice but to withdraw and go on downstairs. Just as usual he had his breakfast and then fed and watered the fowls and let them out of their run. When he got to school, just as usual, the boys called him Henny-penny and enjoyed their joke. The witty boy of the class sacrificed a small chocolate-and-marshmallow egg by putting it on William's chair just before he sat down. School was hateful to William – as hateful as Aunt Rosa's house.

After school, Aunt Rosa had William's tea ready for him. 'I'll just wash my hands upstairs in the bathroom,' he said.

'No, you can do it at the kitchen sink. And, after your tea, I've a job for you.'

And, after his tea, she said: 'Today you can change the straw in the hen-house for me.'

'Now?'

'Yes, now!'

'Shouldn't I go and change out of my school-clothes first?' asked William.

Aunt Rosa stared at him suspiciously. 'You're not usually so fussy . . .'

William waited.

'All right then,' said his aunt. 'Change, but be quick about it. I'll be getting you the barrow and the shovel out of the shed.'

She went into the garden, followed by Bessy; and William went swiftly upstairs. The door of his aunt's room was shut, but he opened it without hesitation. He knew he was safe, for he could hear the rattle of the wheelbarrow down the garden as his aunt manoeuvred it out of the shed; and Bessy would be there with her, too.

The gold chain had not been put away: it lay just as before on the top of the dressing-table. He felt like crying as he picked it up; he had so longed to have it.

He disturbed nothing else, and shut his aunt's bedroom door as he left. Then he went on to his own room. One hand held the gold chain – he would not put it down for an instant; with the other hand he burrowed into his suitcase and brought out the nest-egg. He turned the egg so that its air-hole was uppermost. Then, with the fingers of his other hand, he found the free end of the gold chain and held it exactly above the air-hole. He began to lower it towards the air-hole, to feed it through; and it went through! He had foreseen correctly: the size was right.

He went on dropping the gold chain, link by link, through the air-hole of the nest-egg. The links fell and fell and fell until there were no more, and the whole chain had disappeared inside the nest-egg; and still the egg was not full. He shook the nest-egg, and he could hear the supple chain shifting and settling inside its new home.

'William!' his aunt shouted from the garden. He put the nest-egg into his pocket and then had to take it out again, because he had forgotten that he was supposed to be changing into rough clothes. He changed quickly and, with the nest-egg in a pocket, went down to the job in the hen-house. 'For goodness' sake, boy!' said his aunt. 'I thought you were never coming! Here's the barrow and shovel. Clean the shed right out and barrow the soiled straw to the compost heap. Then fresh straw from the shed. I want to see the job well done. Oh – and mind the nest-egg!'

She left him to his work. The re-strawing took some time, but William did well. His aunt had grudgingly to admit that, when she inspected the inside of the hen-house. She also noted the presence of the nest-egg, just where it should be.

And William left it there.

Aunt Rosa's discovery of the loss of the gold chain was not made until the following morning. William was woken by his aunt shaking him. 'I know you've taken it!' she was crying. 'You've stolen my gold chain!' Bessy stood in the doorway of the bedroom, watching the scene and growling softly.

William managed to say: 'I haven't stolen it.'

Of course, she did not believe him. She turned out all the pockets of his clothes. She unpacked his suitcase all over the floor. She took the mattress and all the bedding off the bedstead and searched them. She searched everywhere; and all the time she ranted at him and cuffed him and slapped him.

It was not more than William had expected, but it was hard to bear. Doggedly, he repeated, 'I haven't stolen it.'

He was late for school, of course, and he had to deliver a

letter from his aunt to the headmaster. Later, the head-master summoned him. 'William, do you know what was in the letter from your aunt?'

'About me?' said William. 'I can guess.'

The headmaster sighed. He said: 'I have written a note in reply to your aunt. I have suggested a time when she can call on me to discuss – things. William, you must be sure to deliver this note to your aunt; she is expecting to hear from me . . .'

The other boys were curious about William's interview with the headmaster. He told them nothing. The witty boy suggested that the head had noticed feathers beginning to sprout on Henny-penny's legs. This boy found two sparrow feathers in the playground and stuck them in William's hair when he was not looking.

At the end of the school day, William took the head-master's note with him back to Aunt Rosa's house; but Aunt Rosa was out. There was a message for him on the kitchen table saying that there was no tea for him today, and that she would be back during the evening.

He did not mind about the food; but – later – he did mind about not being able to get into his bedroom. Bessy lay along the threshold, watching him and growling. She would not let him pass. He said aloud: 'You don't want me here; but I don't want to be here. So we're quits.' That made him feel better about Bessy.

He took the headmaster's note from his pocket, put it on the floor and pushed it with his foot towards Bessy. She seized it angrily in her teeth and tore it into shreds.

He went downstairs and into the garden, to the bottom of it. All the hens were out in the orchard, and he could see the cockerel among them. He went to the hen-house, opened the door and looked in. The fresh straw smelled pleasantly, and there was his dear nest-egg . . .

He stooped and crept inside the hen-house, and pulled the door after him as closely shut as possible. He fumbled in the straw for the nest-egg and found it, and shook it gently, to hear the comforting sound of the chain moving inside.

He settled in the fresh straw on the far side of the hen-house from the roosting perch. At first he sat there; then, beginning to feel drowsy, he lay down in the straw. He fell asleep with the nest-egg up to his cheek.

He slept deeply, dreamlessly, and better than he had ever slept in Aunt Rosa's house.

So he never noticed the fading of daylight, and the hens and cockerel that came stooping in through their pop-hole, into the hen-house for the night. They saw William there, and were disturbed at the sight; but he made no movement or sound, and they reassured themselves. One by one they flew up on the perch, and roosted there, and slept.

He never heard later the voice of his Aunt Rosa calling distractedly up and down the garden and in the orchard, as she had already done inside the house. Neighbours were consulted and gave advice; at last the police were summoned; there was a great deal of telephoning. William slept through it all, his nest-egg to his face.

With the first of daylight the hens and cockerel left the hen-house for the run, and then – since no one had thought of shutting them up last night – for the orchard. The cockerel often stopped to crow, but William did not hear him. He slept on.

The sun was high in the sky before William woke. At first he did not remember where he was. In his own old room at home? In Aunt Rosa's cold house? Neither. He was in a *hen-house*: he had slept there, the whole night through, with the hens and with his old enemy, the cockerel. He laughed aloud. He felt light-hearted, as he had not done for many weeks. He also felt very hungry.

The hens and cockerel had gone; it was time for him to go, too. He did not know what was going to happen next, but at least he had had a long night's sleep in freedom; and he had his precious nest egg safe in his pocket.

He let himself out of the hen-house. He began walking up the garden path towards the house – towards Aunt Rosa's house. As he came nearer, his spirits sank lower. He was walking towards a prison.

Aunt Rosa would be waiting for him. And there she was –
a figure standing on the garden doorstep; and – but no! It
was not his Aunt Rosa. It was his father.

With a wild cry William ran into his father's arms, and
his father picked him up and hugged him safe. 'William!
William!' he repeated, over and over again.

It was some time before any scolding began: 'Why on
earth did you run away? You bad boy – you silly boy! Where
did you go! Your aunt was out of her mind with worry, so
she telephoned me and I drove all through the night to
come. William, you should never, never have run away like
that!'

'But I didn't run away,' said William. 'I was here all the
time.'

'Where?'

'Just in the hen-house at the bottom of the garden.'

William's father began to laugh. 'And you've straw all
over your clothes!'

He took his son indoors to Aunt Rosa – Aunt Rosa,
sleep-starved, haggard with many fears, and by now, fortunately, speechless with fatigue. He explained that William
was back. ('But I've never been away,' protested William.
'The hen-house isn't away.')

William's father said that, now he was here, he might as
well take William off Aunt Rosa's hands. She nodded. It
wasn't that he wasn't grateful to her – Aunt Rosa nodded
again – but he needed his son to be with him, after all.
William was all he had now. 'And somehow we'll manage,'
said William's father. 'I'm not sure how, but we shall
manage.'

Then Aunt Rosa said she was going to bed; and she went,
with Bessy following her. Bessy had had an extraordinarily
disagreeable night, with upsets and unwanted visitors.

William's father telephoned the police and told the
neighbours about William's return. Then he took over
Aunt Rosa's kitchen and made an enormous breakfast for
himself and William. After that, they packed everything
into William's suitcase, got into the car, and drove off. They

did not wake Aunt Rosa to say goodbye, but William's father left a note on the kitchen table.

When the car had taken them well away from Aunt Rosa's house, William said: 'I liked her hen-house and her hens.'

His father said: 'But Rosa said you were frightened of the cockerel.'

'I was afraid of him,' said William, 'but I liked him, too. He was only fierce when he was defending his hens, his family.'

His father glanced down at something William had just taken out of his pocket. 'Did Rosa give you that dummy egg?'

'No,' said William. 'I took it.'

His father frowned. 'That's stealing.'

'I just *needed* it.'

'It's still stealing. You'll have to send it back.'

'It might break in the post. Couldn't we send the money instead?' William had a brilliant idea. 'You could stop it out of my pocket money, and you could tell Aunt Rosa that. That would really please her.'

So it was settled. But, after a while, hesitantly, William asked, 'Did Aunt Rosa ever say I'd stolen anything?'

'No,' his father said, quite positively. 'But then, she didn't know about this egg, did she?'

William thought: She'd tell the headmaster; but she wouldn't dare tell my dad about the chain. Because he knew it was my mum's, and I'd given it to my mum. I wasn't stealing. I just took back.

He tilted the egg in his hands, to feel the movement inside it. He said: 'I shall always keep this egg. On my mantelpiece.'

'You do that,' said his father. 'Only we shall have to find somewhere to live with a room with a mantelpiece in it.'

'We'll manage somehow,' William said comfortably. 'You said so.'

THEODORE TAYLOR

The Cay

The year is 1942. Far from war-torn Europe, German submarines hunt down enemy vessels in the shark-infested waters of the Caribbean. A passenger ship is torpedoed; on board an American boy suffers a violent blow to the head and loses consciousness. Twelve-year-old Phillip wakes up to find himself on a makeshift raft with a cat and the old black sailor who has saved his life. But the boy's injuries soon leave him blind.

Old Timothy, the sailor, never went to school, but understands the ocean, the Cay Islands and the boy as if they were part of him. While he teaches Phillip to survive on a wild, uninhabited island, the blind boy learns that their differences are only skin deep. By the time a new danger strikes out of the blue, he has discovered that you don't need eyes to know a person as they really are . . .

ONE VERY HOT MORNING in July, we were down on north beach where Timothy had found a patch of calico scallops not too far offshore. It was the hottest day we'd ever had on the cay. So hot that each breath felt like fire. And for once, the trade wind was not blowing. Nothing on the cay seemed to be moving.

North beach was a very strange beach anyway. The sand on it felt coarser to my feet. Everything about it felt different, but that didn't really make sense since it was only about a mile from south beach.

Timothy explained, 'D'nawth is alles d'bleak beach on any islan',' but he couldn't say why.

He had just brought some calico scallops ashore when we heard the rifle shot. He came quickly to my side, saying, 'Dat b'trouble.'

Trouble? I thought it meant someone had found the cay. That wasn't trouble. Excited, I asked, 'Who's shooting?'

'D'sea,' he said.

I laughed at him, 'The sea can't shoot a rifle.'

'A crack like d'rifle,' he said, worry in his voice. 'It can make d'shot all right, all right. It b'tell us a veree bad starm is comin', Phill-eep. A tempis'.'

I couldn't quite believe that. However, there had been, distinctly, a crack like a rifle or pistol shot.

He said anxiously, 'D'waves do it. Somewhar far off, out beyond d'Grenadines, or in dat pesky bight off Honduras, a hurrican' is spawnin', young bahss. I feel it. What we heeard was a wave passin' dis lil' hombug point.'

I heard him sniffing the air as if he could smell the hurricane coming. Without the wind, there was a breathless silence around our cay. The sea, he told me, was smooth as green jelly. But already, the water was getting cloudy. There were no birds in sight. The sky, he said, had a yellowish cast to it.

'Come along, we 'ave much to do. D'calico scallop can wait dey own self till after d'tempis'.'

We went up to our hill.

Now I knew why he had chosen the highest point of land on the cay for our hut. Even so, I thought, the waves might tumble over it.

The first thing Timothy did was to lash our water keg high on a palm trunk. Next he took the remaining rope that we had and tied it securely around the same sturdy tree. 'In case d'tempis' reach dis high, lock your arms ovah d'rope an' hang on, Phill-eep.'

I realized then why he had used our rope sparingly; why he had made my guideline down to east beach from vines instead of rope. Every day, I learned of something new that Timothy had done so we could survive.

During the afternoon, he told me this was a freak storm, because most did not come until September or October. August, sometimes. Seldom in July. 'But dis year, d'sea be angry wid all d'death upon it. D'wahr.'

The storms bred, Timothy said, in the eastern North Atlantic, south of the Cape Verde Islands, in the fall, but sometimes, when they were freaks, and early, they bred much closer, in a triangle way off the north-east tip of

South America. Once in a great while, in June or July, they sometimes made up not far from Providencia and San Andrés. Near us. The June ones were only pesky, but the July ones were dangerous.

'Dis be a western starm, I b'guessin'. Dey outrageous strong when dey come,' he said.

Even Stew Cat was nervous. He was around my legs whenever I moved. I asked Timothy what we should do to protect him. He laughed. 'Stew Cat b'go up d'palm on d'lee side iffen it b'gettin' too terrible. Don' worry 'bout Stew Cat.'

Yet I could not help worrying. The thought of losing either of them was unbearable. If something bad happened on the cay, I wanted it to happen to all of us.

Nothing changed during the afternoon, although it seemed to get even hotter. Timothy spent a lot of time down at the raft, stripping off everything usable and carrying it back up the hill. He said we might never see it again, or else it might wash up the hill so that it would be impossible to launch.

Timothy was not purposely trying to frighten me about the violence of the storm; he was just being honest. He had good reason to be frightened himself.

'In '28, I be on d'*Hettie Redd* sout' o' Antigua when d'tempis' hit. D'wind was outrageous, an' d'ol' schooner break up like chips fallin' 'fore d'axe. I wash ashore from d'sea, so wild no mahn believe it. No odder mahn from d'*Hettie Redd* live 'ceptin' me.'

I knew that wild sea from long ago was much on Timothy's mind all afternoon.

We had a huge meal late in the day, much bigger than usual, because Timothy said we might not be able to eat for several days. We had fish and coconut meat, and we each drank several cups of coconut milk. Timothy said that the fish might not return to the reef for at least a week. He'd noticed that they'd already gone to deep water.

After we ate, Timothy carefully cleaned his knife and put

it into the tin box, which he lashed high on the same tree that held our water keg.

'We ready, Phill-eep,' he said.

At sunset, with the air heavy and hot, Timothy described the sky to me. He said it was flaming red and that there were thin veils of high clouds. It was so still over our cay that we could hear nothing but the rustling of the lizards.

Just before dark, Timothy said, ''Twon't be long now, Phill-eep.'

We felt a light breeze that began to ripple the smooth sea. Timothy said he saw an arc of very black clouds to the west. They looked as though they were beginning to join the higher clouds.

I gathered Stew Cat close to me as we waited, feeling the warm breeze against my face. Now and then, there were gusts of wind that rattled the palm fronds, shaking the little hut.

It was well after dark when the first drops of rain spattered the hut, and with them, the wind turned cool. When it gusted, the rain hit the hut like handfuls of gravel.

Then the wind began to blow steadily, and Timothy went out of the hut to look up at the sky. He shouted, 'Dey boilin' ovah now, Phill-eep. 'Tis hurrican', to be sure.'

We could hear the surf beginning to crash as the wind drove waves before it, and Timothy ducked back inside to stand in the opening of the hut, his big body stretched so that he could hang on to the overhead frame, keeping the hut erect as long as possible.

I felt movement around my legs and feet. Things were slithering. I screamed to Timothy who shouted back, 'B'nothin' but d'lil' lizzard, comin' high groun'.'

Rain was now slashing into the hut, and the wind was reaching a steady howl. The crash of the surf sounded closer; I wondered if it was already beginning to push up towards our hill. The rain was icy, and I was wet, head to foot. I was shivering, but more from the thought of the sea rolling over us than from the sudden cold.

In a moment, there was a splintering sound, and Timothy dropped down beside me, covering my body with his. Our hut had blown away. He shouted, 'Phill-eep, put your 'ead downg.' I rolled over on my stomach, my cheek against the wet sand. Stew Cat burrowed down between us.

There was no sound now except the roar of the storm. Even the sound of the wind was being beaten down by the wildness of the sea. The rain was hitting my back like thousands of hard berries blown from air guns.

Once something solid hit us and then rolled on. 'Sea grape,' Timothy shouted. It was being torn up by the roots.

We stayed flat on the ground for almost two hours, taking the storm's punishment, barely able to breathe in the driving rain. Then Timothy shouted hoarsely, 'To d'palm.'

The sea was beginning to reach for our hilltop, climbing the forty feet with raging whitecaps. Timothy dragged me towards the palm. I held Stew Cat against my chest.

Standing with his back to the storm, Timothy put my arms through the loops of rope, and then roped himself, behind me, to the tree.

Soon, I felt water around my ankles. Then it washed to my knees. It would go back and then crash against us again. Timothy was taking the full blows of the storm, sheltering me with his body. When the water receded, it would tug at us, and Timothy's strength would fight against it. I could feel the steel in his arms as the water tried to suck us away.

Even in front of him, crushed against the trunk of the palm, I could feel the rain, which was now jabbing into me like the punches of a nail. It was not falling towards earth but being driven straight ahead by the wind.

We must have been against the palm for almost an hour when suddenly the wind died down and the rain became gentle. Timothy panted, 'D'eye! We can relax a bit till d'odder side o' d'tempis' hit us.'

I remembered that hurricanes, which are great circling storms, have a calm eye in the centre.

'Are you all right?' I asked.

He replied hoarsely, 'I b'damp, but all right.'

Yet I heard him making small noises, as if it were painful to move, as we stood back from the palm trunk. We sat down on the ground beside it, still being pelted with rain, to wait for the eye to pass. Water several inches deep swirled around us, but was not tugging at us.

It was strange and eerie in the eye of the hurricane. I knew we were surrounded on all sides by violent winds, but the little cay was calm and quiet. I reached over for Timothy. He was cradling his head in his arms, still making those small noises, like a hurt animal.

In twenty or thirty minutes, the wind picked up sharply and Timothy said that we must stand against the palm again. Almost within seconds, the full fury of the storm hit the cay once more. Timothy pressed me tightly against the rough bark.

It was even worse this time, but I do not remember everything that happened. We had been there awhile when a wave that must have reached half-way up the palms crashed against us. The water went way over my head. I choked and struggled. Then another giant wave struck us. I lost consciousness then. Timothy did, too, I think.

When I came to, the wind had died down, coming at us only in gusts. The water was still washing around our ankles, but seemed to be going back into the sea now. Timothy was still behind me, but he felt cold and limp. He was sagging, his head down on my shoulder.

'Timothy, wake up,' I said.

He did not answer.

Using my shoulders, I tried to shake him, but the massive body did not move. I stood very still to see if he was breathing. I could feel his stomach moving and I reached over my shoulder to his mouth. There was air coming out. I knew that he was not dead.

However, Stew Cat was gone.

I worked for a few minutes to release my arms from the loops of rope around the palm trunk, and then slid out from under Timothy's body. He slumped lifelessly against the palm. I felt along the ropes that bound his forearms to the trunk until I found the knots.

With his weight against them, it was hard to pull them loose, even though they were sailor's knots and had loops in them. The rope was soaked, which made it worse.

I must have worked for half an hour before I had him free from the trunk. He fell backwards into the wet sand, and lay there moaning. I knew there was very little I could do for him except to sit by him in the light rain, holding his hand. In my world of darkness, I had learned that holding a hand could be like medicine.

After a long while, he seemed to recover. His first words, painful and dragged out, were, 'Phill-eep . . . you . . . all right . . . be true?'

'I'm OK, Timothy,' I said.

He said weakly, 'Terrible tempis'.'

He must have rolled over on his stomach in the sand, because his hand left mine abruptly. Then he went to sleep, I guess.

I touched his back. It felt warm and sticky. I ran my hand lightly down it, suddenly realizing that I, too, was completely naked. The wind and sea had torn our tatters of clothes from us.

Timothy had been cut to ribbons by the wind, which drove the rain and tiny grains of sand before it. It had flayed his back and his legs until there were very few places that weren't cut. He was bleeding, but there was nothing I could do to stop it. I found his hard, horny hand again, wrapped mine around it, and lay down beside him.

I went to sleep too.

Sometime long after dawn, I awakened. The rain had stopped, and the wind had died down to its usual whisper. But I think the clouds were still covering the sky because I could not feel the sun.

I said, 'Timothy,' but he did not answer me. His hand was cold and stiff in mine.

Old Timothy, of Charlotte Amalie, was dead.

I stayed there beside him for a long time, very tired,

thinking that he should have taken me with him wherever he had gone. I did not cry then. There are times when you are beyond tears.

I went back to sleep, and this time when I awakened, I heard a meow. Then I cried for a long time, holding Stew Cat tight. Aside from him, I was blind and alone on a forgotten cay.

FRANCES HODGSON BURNETT

The Secret Garden

Mary Lennox may have grown up in far away India with servants granting her every wish, but no one loves her. She lives in a world of her own, not interested in other people. Then, suddenly, her parents die.

Mary doesn't have a friend to call her own until she comes to live in the house of an uncle she has never met, on the Yorkshire moors. With her uncle away, and his grand old house gloomy and silent, it takes the Sowerby family living in a simple cottage on the moors, and the promise of spring in a secret garden, to breathe new life into her unhappy world.

Martha Sowerby works as a maid in the house, Dickon is her twelve-year-old brother, and Ben Weatherstaff is a lonely old gardener who works in the rambling, mysterious grounds. Here, Mary takes Dickon into her secret garden for the first time . . .

FOR TWO OR THREE MINUTES he stood looking round him, while Mary watched him, and then he began to walk about softly, even more lightly than Mary had walked the first time she had found herself inside the four walls. His eyes seemed to be taking in everything – the grey trees with the grey creepers climbing over them and hanging from their branches, the tangle on the wall and among the grass, the evergreen alcoves with the stone seats and tall flower urns standing in them.

'I never thought I'd see this place,' he said at last in a whisper.

'Did you know about it?' asked Mary.

She had spoken aloud and he made a sign to her.

'We must talk low,' he said, 'or someone'll hear us an' wonder what's to do in here.'

'Oh! I forgot!' said Mary, feeling frightened and putting her hand quickly against her mouth. 'Did you know about the garden?' she asked again when she had recovered herself.

Dickon nodded.

'Martha told me there was one as no one ever went inside,' he answered. 'Us used to wonder what it was like.'

He stopped and looked round at the lovely grey tangle about him, and his round eyes looked queerly happy.

'Eh! The nests as'll be here come springtime,' he said. 'It'd be th' safest nestin' place in England. No one ever comin' near an' tangles o' trees an' roses to build in. I wonder all th' birds on th' moor don't build here.'

Mistress Mary put her hand on his arm again without knowing it.

'Will there be roses?' she whispered. 'Can you tell? I thought perhaps they were all dead.'

'Eh! No! Not them – not all of 'em!' he answered. 'Look here!'

He stepped over to the nearest tree – an old, old one with grey lichen all over its bark, but upholding a curtain of tangled sprays and branches. He took a thick knife out of his pocket and opened one of its blades.

'There's lots o' dead wood as ought to be cut out,' he said. 'An' there's a lot o' old wood, but it made some new last year. This here's a new bit,' and he touched a shoot which looked brownish-green instead of hard, dry grey.

Mary touched it herself in an eager, reverent way.

'That one?' she said. 'Is that one quite alive – quite?'

Dickon curved his wide, smiling mouth.

'It's as wick as you or me,' he said; and Mary remembered that Martha had told her that 'wick' meant 'alive' or 'lively'.

'I'm glad it's wick!' she cried out in her whisper. 'I want them all to be wick. Let us go round the garden and count how many wick ones there are.'

She quite panted with eagerness, and Dickon was as eager as she was. They went from tree to tree and from bush to bush. Dickon carried his knife in his hand and showed her things which she thought wonderful.

'They're run wild,' he said, 'but th' strongest ones has fair thrived on it. The delicatest ones has died out, but the others has growed an' growed, an' spread an' spread, till they's a wonder. See here!' and he pulled down a thick, grey, dry-looking branch. 'A body might think this was dead wood, but I don't believe it is – down to th' root. I'll cut it low down an' see.'

He knelt and with his knife cut the lifeless-looking branch through, not far above the earth.

'There!' he said exultantly. 'I told thee so. There's green in that wood yet. Look at it.'

Mary was down on her knees before he spoke, gazing with all her might.

'When it looks a bit greenish an' juicy like that, it's wick,' he explained. 'When th' inside is dry an' breaks easy, like this here piece I've cut off, it's done for. There's a big root here as all this live wood sprung out of, an' if th' old wood's cut off an' it's dug round, an' took care of there'll be' – he stopped and lifted his face to look up at the climbing and hanging sprays about him – 'there'll be a fountain o' roses here this summer.'

They went from bush to bush and from tree to tree. He was very strong and clever with his knife and knew how to cut the dry and dead wood away, and could tell when an unpromising bough or twig had still green life in it. In the course of half an hour, Mary thought she could tell too, and when he cut through a lifeless-looking branch she would cry out joyfully under her breath when she caught sight of the least shade of moist green. The spade, and hoe, and fork were very useful. He showed her how to use the fork while he dug about the roots with the spade and stirred the earth and let the air in.

They were working industriously round one of the biggest standard roses when he caught sight of something which made him utter an exclamation of surprise.

'Why!' he cried, pointing to the grass a few feet away. 'Who did that?'

It was one of Mary's own little clearings round the pale-green points.

'I did it,' said Mary.

'Why, I thought tha' didn't know nothin' about gardenin',' he exclaimed.

'I don't,' she answered, 'but they were so little and the grass was so thick and strong, and they looked as if they had no room to breathe. So I made a place for them. I don't even know what they are.'

Dickon went and knelt down by them, smiling his wide smile.

'Tha' was right,' he said. 'A gardener couldn't have told thee better. They'll grow now like Jack's bean-stalk. They're crocuses an' snowdrops, an' these here is narcissuses,' turning to another patch, 'an' here's daffydown-dillys. Eh! They will be a sight.'

He ran from one clearing to another.

'Tha' has done a lot o' work for such a little wench,' he said, looking her over.

'I'm growing fatter,' said Mary, 'and I'm growing stronger. I used always to be tired. When I dig I'm not tired at all. I like to smell the earth when it's turned up.'

'It's rare good for thee,' he said, nodding his head wisely. 'There's naught as nice as th' smell o' good clean earth, except th' smell o' fresh growin' things when th' rain falls on 'em. I get out on th' moor many a day when it's rainin' an' I lie under a bush an' listen to th' soft swish o' drops on th' heather an' I just sniff an' sniff. My nose end fair quivers like a rabbit's, Mother says.'

'Do you never catch cold?' inquired Mary, gazing at him wonderingly. She had never seen such a funny boy, or such a nice one.

'Not me,' he said, grinning. 'I never ketched cold since I was born. I wasn't brought up nesh enough. I've chased about th' moor in all weathers, same as th' rabbits does. Mother says I've sniffed too much fresh air for twelve year' to ever get to sniffin' with cold. I'm as tough as a white thorn knobstick.'

He was working all the time he was talking and Mary was following him and helping him with her fork or the trowel.

'There's a lot of work to do here!' he said once, looking about quite exultantly.

'Will you come again and help me to do it?' Mary begged. 'I'm sure I can help, too. I can dig and pull up weeds, and do whatever you tell me. Oh! do come, Dickon!'

'I'll come every day if tha' wants me, rain or shine,' he answered stoutly. 'It's th' best fun I ever had in my life – shut in here an' wakening' up a garden.'

'If you will come,' said Mary, 'if you will help me to make it alive I'll – I don't know what I'll do,' she ended helplessly. What could you do for a boy like that?

'I'll tell thee what tha'll do,' said Dickon, with his happy grin. 'Tha'll get fat an' tha'll get as hungry as a young fox an' tha'll learn how to talk to th' robin same as I do. Eh! We'll have a lot o' fun.'

He began to walk about, looking up in the trees and at the walls and bushes with a thoughtful expression.

'I wouldn't want to make it look like a gardener's garden, all clipped an' spick an' span, would you?' he said. 'It's nicer like this with things runnin' wild, an' swingin' an' catchin' hold of each other.'

'Don't let us make it tidy,' said Mary anxiously. 'It wouldn't seem like a secret garden if it was tidy.'

Dickon stood rubbing his rusty-red head with a rather puzzled look.

'It's a secret garden sure enough,' he said, 'but seems like someone besides th' robin must have been in it since it was shut up ten year' ago.'

'But the door was locked and the key was buried,' said Mary. 'No one could get in.'

'That's true,' he answered. 'It's a queer place. Seems to me as if there'd been a bit o' prunin' done here an' there, later than ten year' ago.'

'But how could it have been done?' said Mary.

He was examining a branch of a standard rose and he shook his head.

'Aye! How could it!' he murmured. 'With th' door locked an' th' key buried.'

Mistress Mary always felt that however many years she lived she should never forget that first morning when her garden began to grow. Of course, it did seem to begin to grow for her that morning. When Dickon began to clear places to plant seeds, she remembered what Basil had sung at her when he wanted to tease her.

'Are there any flowers that look like bells?' she inquired.

'Lilies o' th' valley does,' he answered, digging away with the trowel, 'an' there's Canterbury bells, an' campanulas.'

'Let us plant some,' said Mary.

'There's lilies o' th' valley here already; I saw 'em. They'll have growed too close an' we'll have to separate 'em, but there's plenty. Th' other ones take two years to bloom from seed, but I can bring you some bits o' plants from our cottage garden. Why does tha' want 'em?'

Then Mary told him about Basil and his brothers and sisters in India and of how she had hated them, and of their calling her 'Mistress Mary Quite Contrary'.

'They used to dance round and sing at me. They sang:

> *Mistress Mary, quite contrary,*
> *How does your garden grow?*
> *With silver bells and cockle shells,*
> *And marigolds all in a row.*

I just remembered it and it made me wonder if there were really flowers like silver bells.'

She frowned a little and gave her trowel a rather spiteful dig into the earth.

'I wasn't as contrary as they were.'

But Dickon laughed.

'Eh!' he said, and as he crumpled the rich black soil she saw he was sniffing up the scent of it, 'there doesn't seem to be no need for no one to be contrary when there's flowers an' such like, an' such lots o' friendly wild things runnin' about makin' homes for themselves, or buildin' nests an' singin' an' whistling, does there?'

Mary, kneeling by him holding the seeds, looked at him and stopped frowning.

'Dickon,' she said. 'You are as nice as Martha said you were. I like you, and you make the fifth person. I never thought I should like five people.'

Dickon sat up on his heels as Martha did when she was polishing the grate. He did look funny and delightful, Mary thought, with his round blue eyes and red cheeks and happy-looking turned-up nose.

'Only five folks as tha' likes?' he said. 'Who is th' other four?'

'Your mother and Martha,' Mary checked them off on her fingers, 'and the robin and Ben Weatherstaff.'

Dickon laughed, so that he was obliged to stifle the sound by putting his arm over his mouth.

'I know tha' thinks I'm a queer lad,' he said, 'but I think tha' art th' queerest little lass I ever saw.'

Then Mary did a strange thing. She leaned forward and asked him a question she had never dreamed of asking anyone before. And she tried to ask it in Yorkshire because that was his language, and in India a native was always pleased if you knew his speech.

'Does tha' like me?' she said.

'Eh!' he answered heartily, 'that I does. I likes thee wonderful, an' so does th' robin, I do believe!'

'That's two, then,' said Mary. 'That's two for me.'

And then they began to work harder than ever and more joyful. Mary was startled and sorry when she heard the big clock in the courtyard strike the hour of her midday dinner.

'I shall have to go,' she said mournfully. 'And you will have to go too, won't you?'

Dickon grinned.

'My dinner's easy to carry about with me,' he said. 'Mother always lets me put a bit o' somethin' in my pocket.'

He picked up his coat from the grass and brought out of a pocket a lumpy little bundle tied up in a quite clean, coarse, blue and white handkerchief. It held two thick pieces of bread with a slice of something laid between them.

'It's oftenest naught but bread,' he said, 'but I've got a fine slice o' fat bacon with it today.'

Mary thought it looked a queer dinner, but he seemed ready to enjoy it.

'Run on an' get thy victuals,' he said. 'I'll be done with mine first. I'll get some more work done before I start back home.'

He sat down with his back against a tree.

'I'll call th' robin up,' he said, 'and give him th' rind o' th' bacon to peck at. They likes a bit o' fat wonderful.'

Mary could scarcely bear to leave him. Suddenly it seemed as if he might be a sort of wood fairy who might be gone when she came into the garden again. He seemed too good to be true. She went slowly half-way to the door in the wall and then she stopped and went back.

'Whatever happens, you – you never would tell?' she said.

His poppy-coloured cheeks were distended with his first big bite of bread and bacon, but he managed to smile encouragingly.

'If tha' was a missel thrush an' showed me where thy nest was, does tha' think I'd tell anyone? Not me,' he said. 'Tha' art as safe as a missel thrush.'

And she was quite sure she was.

JAMES VANCE MARSHALL

Walkabout

The Aboriginal people of Australia have always
known that everything in Nature is linked with
everything else. Land, sky and water; trees,
animals and people; all things on the planet are
part of one family.

In this story, an American girl and her young
brother are the only survivors of a plane crash
in the Australian desert. Mary and Peter have
grown up in a world of shops, houses and cars,
and have never had to learn how to stay alive.
Now they face hunger, thirst and exhaustion.
They have not grown up to feel part of the
natural world at all, and so they feel *apart* from
it. They have also been taught to look down on
people of different races.

The children are found lost and helpless by
an aboriginal boy who lives in harmony with
this great wilderness that his people have left
unchanged for many thousands of years . . . .

THE GIRL'S FIRST IMPULSE was to grab Peter and run; but as her eyes swept over the stranger, her fear died slowly away. The boy was young – certainly no older than she was; he was unarmed, and his attitude was more inquisitive than threatening: more puzzled than hostile.

He wasn't the least bit like an African Negro. His skin was certainly black, but beneath it was a curious hint of undersurface bronze, and it was fine-grained: glossy, satiny, almost silk-like. His hair wasn't crinkly but nearly straight; and his eyes were blue-black: big, soft and inquiring. In his hand was a baby rock wallaby, its eyes, unclosed in death, staring vacantly above a tiny pointed snout.

All this Mary noted and accepted. The thing that she couldn't accept, the thing that seemed to her shockingly and indecently wrong, was the fact that the boy was naked.

The three children stood looking at each other in the middle of the Australian desert. Motionless as the outcrops of granite they stared, and stared, and stared. Between them the distance was less than the spread of an outstretched arm, but more than a hundred thousand years.

Brother and sister were products of the highest strata of humanity's evolution. In them the primitive had long ago been swept aside, been submerged by mechanization, been swamped by scientific development, been nullified by the standardized pattern of the white man's way of life. They had climbed a long way up the ladder of progress; they had climbed so far, in fact, that they had forgotten how their climb had started. Coddled in babyhood, psychoanalysed in childhood, nourished on pre-digested patent foods, provided with continuous push-button entertainment, the basic realities of life were something they'd never had to face.

It was very different with the Aboriginal. He knew what reality was. He led a way of life that was already old when Tutankhamun started to build his tomb; a way of life that had been tried and proved before the white man's continents were even lifted out of the sea. Among the secret water-holes of the Australian desert his people had lived and died, unchanged and unchanging, for twenty thousand years. Their lives were unbelievably simple. They had no homes, no crops, no clothes, no possessions. The few things they had, they shared: food and wives; children and laughter; tears and hunger and thirst. They walked from one water-hole to the next; they exhausted one supply of food, then moved on to another. Their lives were utterly uncomplicated because they were devoted to one purpose, dedicated in their entirety to the waging of one battle: the battle with death. Death was their ever-present enemy. He sought them out from every dried-up salt pan, from the flames of every bush fire. He was never far away. Keeping him at bay was the Aboriginals' full-time job: the job they'd been doing for twenty thousand years: the job they were good at.

The desert sun streamed down. The children stared and stared.

Mary had decided not to move. To move would be a sign of weakness. She remembered being told about the man who'd come face to face with a lion, and had stared it out, had caused it to slink discomfited away. That was what she'd do to the black boy; she'd stare at him until he felt the shame of his nakedness and slunk away. She thrust out her chin, and glared.

Peter had decided to take his cue from his sister. Clutching her hand he stood waiting: waiting for something to happen.

The Aboriginal was in no hurry. Time had little value to him. His next meal – the rock wallaby – was assured. Water was near. Tomorrow was also a day. For the moment he was content to examine these strange creatures at his leisure. Their clumsy, lumbering movements intrigued him; their lack of weapons indicated their harmlessness. His eyes moved slowly, methodically from one to another: examining them from head to foot. They were the first white people a member of his tribe had ever seen.

Mary, beginning to resent this scrutiny, intensified her glare. But the bush boy seemed in no way perturbed; his appraisal went methodically on.

After a while Peter started to fidget. The delay was fraying his nerves. He wished someone would do something: wished something would happen. Then, quite involuntarily, he himself started a new train of events. His head began to waggle; his nose tilted skywards; he spluttered and choked; he tried to hold his breath; but all in vain. It had to come. He sneezed.

It was a mighty sneeze for such a little fellow: the release of a series of concatenated explosions, all the more violent for having been dammed back.

To his sister the sneeze was a calamity. She had just intensified her stare to the point – she felt sure – of irresistibility, when the spell was shattered. The bush boy's attention shifted from her to Peter.

Frustration warped her sense of justice. She condemned her brother out of court; was turning on him angrily, when a second sneeze, even mightier than the first, shattered the silence of the bush.

Mary raised her eyes to heaven: invoking the gods as witnesses to her despair. But the vehemence of the second sneeze was still tumbling leaves from the humble-bushes, when a new sound made her whirl around. A gust of laughter: melodious laughter; low at first, then becoming louder: unrestrained: disproportionate: uncontrolled.

She looked at the bush boy in amazement. He was doubled up with belly-shaking spasms of mirth.

Peter's incongruous, out-of-proportion sneeze had touched off one of his people's most highly developed traits: a sense of the ridiculous; a sense so keenly felt as to be almost beyond control. The bush boy laughed with complete abandon. He flung himself to the ground. He rolled head over heels in unrestrained delight.

His mirth was infectious. It woke in Peter an instant response: a like appreciation of the ludicrous. The guilt that the little boy had started to feel, melted away. At first apologetically, then whole-heartedly, he too started to laugh.

The barrier of twenty thousand years vanished in the twinkling of an eye.

The boys' laughter echoed back from the granite rocks. They started to strike comic postures, each striving to outdo the other in their grotesque abandon.

Mary watched them. She would have dearly loved to join in. A year ago – in her tomboy days – she would have. But not now. She was too sensible: too grown up. Yet not grown up enough to be free of an instinctive longing to share in the fun: to throw convention to the winds and join the capering jamboree. This longing she repressed. She stood aloof: disapproving. At last she went up to Peter and took his hand.

'That's enough, Peter,' she said.

The skylarking subsided. For a moment there was silence, then the bush boy spoke.

'*Worumgala!*' (Where do you come from?) His voice was lilting as his laughter.

Mary and Peter looked at each other blankly.

The bush boy tried again.

'*Worum mwa!*' (Where are you going?)

It was Peter, not Mary, who floundered into the field of conversation.

'We dunno what you're talking about, darkie. But we're lost, see. We want to go to Adelaide. That's where Uncle Keith lives. Which way do we go?'

The black boy grinned. To him the little one's voice was comic as his appearance: half-gabble, half-chirp; and shrill, like a baby magpie's. Peter grinned back, eager for another orgy of laughter. But the bush boy wanted to be serious now. He stepped noiselessly up to Peter, brushed his fingers over the boy's face, then looked at them expectantly; but to his surprise the whiteness hadn't come off. He ran his fingers through Peter's hair. Again he was surprised; no powdered clay, nor red-ochre paste. He turned his attention to the white boy's clothes.

Peter was by no means perturbed. On the contrary he felt flattered; proud. He realized that the bush boy had never seen anything like him before. He held himself very straight, swelled out his chest, and turned slowly round and round.

The bush boy's dark tapering fingers plucked gently at his shirt, following the line of the seams, testing the strength of the criss-cross weave, exploring the mystery of the buttonholes. Then his attention passed from shirt to shorts. Peter became suddenly loquacious.

'Those are shorts, darkie. Short pants. You oughta have 'em too. To cover your bottom up. Haven't you any shops round here?'

The bush boy refused to be diverted. He had found the broad band of elastic that kept the shorts in place. While he fingered it, the white boy prattled on.

'That's elastic that is; keeps your shorts in place. It stretches. Look!'

He stuck his thumbs into the waistband, pulled the elastic away from his hips, then let it fly back. The resounding smack made the bush boy jump. Thoroughly pleased with himself Peter repeated the performance, this time adding a touch of pantomime, staggering backwards as if he'd been struck. The black boy saw the joke. He grinned, but this time he kept his laughter under control; for his examination was a serious business. He ended up with a detailed inspection of Peter's sandals.

Then he turned to Mary.

It was the moment the girl had been dreading.

Yet she didn't draw back. She wanted to; God alone knew how she wanted to. Her nerves were strung taut. The idea of being manhandled by a naked black boy appalled her: struck at the root of one of the basic principles of her civilized code. It was terrifying; revolting; obscene. Back in Charleston it would have got the darkie lynched. Yet she didn't move; not even when the dark fingers ran like spiders up and down her body.

She stayed motionless because, deep-down, she knew she had nothing to fear. The things that she'd been told way back in Charleston were somehow not applicable any more. The values she'd been taught to cherish became suddenly meaningless. A little guilty, a little resentful, and more than a little bewildered, she waited passively for whatever might happen next.

The bush boy's inspection didn't take long. The larger of these strange creatures, he saw at once, was much the same as the smaller – except that the queer things draped around it were, if possible, even more ludicrous. Almost perfunctorily his fingers ran over Mary's face, frock and sandals; then he stepped back: satisfied. There was nothing more he wanted to know.

Turning to where the dead rock wallaby lay in the sand, he picked it up. Odd ants had found it: were nosing through its fur. The boy brushed them off. Then he walked quietly away; away down the valley; soon he was out of sight.

The children couldn't believe it; couldn't believe that he'd really left them. It was all so sudden: so utterly unexpected.

Peter was first to grasp what had happened.

'Mary!' his voice was frightened. 'He's gone!'

The girl said nothing. She was torn by conflicting emotions. Relief that the naked black boy had disappeared, and regret that she hadn't asked him for help; fear that nobody could help them anyhow, and a sneaking feeling that perhaps if anyone could it had been the black boy. A couple of days ago she'd have known what to do; known what was best; known how to act. But she didn't know now. Uncertain, she hid her face in her hands.

It was Peter who made the decision. In the bush boy's laughter he'd found something he liked: a lifeline he didn't intend to lose.

'Hey, Mary!' he gasped. 'Come on. After him!'

He went crashing into the bush. Slowly, doubtfully, his sister followed.

'Hey, darkie!' Peter's reedy treble echoed down the valley. 'We wanna come too. Wait for us!'

'Hey, darkie!' the rocks re-echoed. 'Wait for us. Wait for us. Wait for us.'

*

THE BUSH BOY TURNED. He knew what the call meant: the strangers were coming after him, were following him down the valley; already he could hear them crashing and lumbering through the scrub.

He waited; relaxed both physically and mentally: one hand passed behind his back and closed round the opposite elbow; one foot, ostrich-like, resting on the calf of the opposite leg. He wasn't frightened, for he knew instinctively that the strangers were harmless as a pair of tail-less kangaroos; but he *was* mildly surprised, for he had thought them both, especially the larger, impatient, eager to be on their way. As the children came racing towards him, he dropped his foot to the ground; became suddenly all attention; full of curiosity to know what they wanted to say and how they were going to say it.

Peter launched into a breathless appeal.

'Hey, don't leave us, darkie! We're lost. We want food, an' drink. And we wanna know how we get to Adelaide.'

Mary looked at the bush boy, and saw in his eyes a gleam of amusement. It angered her, for she knew the cause; Peter's high-pitched, corncrakey voice. All the tenets of progressive society and racial superiority combined inside her to form a deep-rooted core of resentment. It was wrong, cruelly wrong, that she and her brother should be forced to run for help to a Negro; and a naked Negro at that. She clutched Peter's hand, half drawing him away.

But Peter was obsessed by none of his sister's scruples. To him their problem was simple, uncomplicated: they wanted help, and here was someone who could, his instinct told him, provide it. The fact that his appeal had failed to register first time nonplussed him for a moment. But he wasn't put off; he stuck to his guns. Breath and composure regained, he now spoke slowly, in a lower, less excited key.

'Look, darkie, we're lost. We want water. You sabby water? War-tur. War-tur.'

He cupped his hands together, drew them up to his lips, and went through the motions of swallowing. The bush boy nodded.

'*Arkooloola.*'

His eyes were serious now. Understanding. Sympathetic. He knew what it meant to be thirsty.

'*Arkooloola.*'

He said the word again. Softly, musically, like the rippling of water over rock. He pursed up his lips and moved them as though he, too, were drinking.

Peter hopped delightedly from foot to foot.

'That's it, darkie. You've got it. *Arkooloolya.* That's the stuff we want. And food too. You sabby food? Foo-ood. Foo-ood.'

He went through the motions of cutting with knife and fork, then started to champ his jaws.

The cutting meant nothing to the bush boy; but the jaw champing did. Again his eyes were sympathetic.

'*Yeemara.*'

His teeth, in unison with Peter's, clicked in understanding.

The white boy was jubilant.

'You've got it, darkie. Got it first time. *Yeemara* an' *Arkooloolya*. That's the stuff we want. Now where do we get 'em?'

The bush boy turned, moved away at right angles, into the scrub. He paused, glanced over his shoulder, then moved away again.

'*Kurura*,' he said.

There was no mistaking his meaning.

'Come on, Mary,' the boy hissed excitedly. '*Kurura*, that means "follow me".'

He trotted eagerly after the bush boy.

Slowly, reluctantly, the girl followed.

After a while they came to a forest of heartleaves. Beneath the thick, closely-woven foliage the shade was deep: a striking contrast to the glare of the bush. Beneath the close-packed trees the white children moved uncertainly, stumblingly: their sun-narrowed pupils slow to adjust themselves to the sudden darkness. But the bush boy, his eyes refocusing almost at once, pushed rapidly on. The others, stumbling and tripping over ground roots, were hard put to keep up with him.

It was cool beneath the heartleaves; cool and quiet and motionless as a sylvan stage set. Hour after hour the bush boy led on, gliding like a bar of well-oiled shadow among the giant trees. He moved without apparent effort, yet quickly enough for Peter to be forced to jog-trot. Soon the small boy was panting. In spite of the shade, sweat plastered back his hair; trickled round his eyes and into his mouth. He started to lag behind. Seeing him in trouble, Mary also dropped back; and Peter reached for her hand.

The girl was pleased: gratified that in his difficulties he'd turned to her. Subconscious twinges of jealousy had been tormenting her. She had been hurt, deeply hurt, at his so quickly transferring his sense of reliance from her to an

uncivilized and naked black. But now things were returning to normal; now he was coming back to the sisterly
fold.

'All right, Peter,' she whispered, 'we won't leave you
behind.'

She knew that he must – like her – be suffering cruelly
from thirst, hunger, and physical exhaustion: knew that his
mouth, like hers, must feel as if it were crammed with
red-hot cotton wool. But there was nothing they could do
about it: or would it, she wondered, help if they acted like
dogs – lolled out their tongues and panted?

Ahead of them the heartleaves ended abruptly. One
moment they were groping forward in deep shade, the next
they were looking out across an expanse of glaring sand:
mile after shimmering mile of ridge and dune, salt-pan and
iron-rock: the Sturt Desert: heat-hazed, sun-drenched,
waterless.

'*Kurura*,' the bush boy said.

He started to walk into the desert.

Mary held back. She didn't exactly mistrust the bush
boy, didn't doubt that if he wished he could – eventually –
lead them to food and water. But how far away would the
food and water be? Too far, most likely, for them ever to
reach it. She sank to her knees in the shade of the last of the
heartleaves. Peter collapsed beside her; the sweat from his
hair ran damply into the lap of her dress.

The bush boy came back. He spoke softly, urgently, the
pitch of his words rising and falling like the murmur of
wavelets on a sandy shore. The words themselves were
meaningless; but his gestures spoke plainly enough. If they
stayed where they were they would die: the bush boy fell to
the sand, his fingers scrabbling the dry earth; soon the evil
spirits would come to molest their bodies; the bush boy's
eyes rolled in terror. But if they followed him he would take
them to water; the bush boy swallowed and gulped. They
hadn't far to go: only as far as the hill-that-had-fallen-out-
of-the-moon; his finger pointed to a strange outcrop of rock
that rose like a gargantuan cairn out of the desert, a cairn

the base of which was circled by a dark, never-moving shadow.

It looked very far away.

The girl wiped the sweat out of her eyes. In the shade of the heartleaves it was mercifully cool; far cooler than it would be in the desert. It would be so much easier, she thought, to give the struggle up, simply to stay where they were. She looked at the cairn critically. How could the bush boy know there was water there? Whoever heard of finding water on top of a pile of rock in the middle of a desert?

'Arkooloola,' the bush boy insisted. He said it again and again, pointing to the base of the cairn.

The girl looked more closely, shading her eyes against the glare of the sun. She noticed that there was something strange about the shadow at the foot of the cairn. As far as she could see, it went all the way round. It couldn't, then, be ordinary shadow, caused by the sun. What else, she wondered, could create such a circle of shade? The answer came suddenly, in a flood of wonder and disbelief. It must be vegetation. Trees and bushes: thick, luxuriant, verdant, and lush. And such vegetation, she knew, could only spring from continually watered roots. She struggled to her feet.

It seemed a long way to the hill-that-had-fallen-out-of-the-moon. By the time they got there the sun was setting.

They came to the humble-bushes first, the twitching, quivering leaves tumbling to the sand as they approached. Then came the straw-like mellowbane, and growing amongst them a grass of a very different kind: sturdy reed-thick grass, each blade tipped with a black, bean-shaped nodule: rustling death-rattle, astir in the sunset wind. The bush boy snapped off one of the reeds. He drove it into the sand. Its head, when he pulled it out, was damp. He smiled encouragement.

'Arkooloola,' he said, and hurried on.

The base of the cairn rose steeply, strata upon strata of terraced iron-rock rising sheer from the desert floor; and the bottom belt of strata was moss-coated and glistening damp, with lacy maidenhair and filigree spider-fern trailing from every crevice. The children stumbled on, brushing aside the umbrella ferns, spurred forward now by the plash of water and by a sudden freshness in the air.

Peter had been lagging behind – for the last mile Mary had been half-carrying, half-dragging him. But now, like an iron filing drawn to a magnet, he broke loose and went scurrying ahead. He disappeared into the shade of the umbrella ferns, and a second later Mary heard his hoarse, excited shout.

'It's water, Mary! Water.'

'*Arkooloola*,' the bush boy grinned.

Together black boy and white girl pushed through the tangle of fern until they came to a tiny pear-shaped basin carved out of solid rock by the ceaseless drip of water. Beside the basin Peter was flat on his face, his head, almost up to his ears, dunked in the clear translucent pool. In a second Mary was flat out beside him. Both children drank, and drank, and drank.

The water was lukewarm; for though the sun was no longer shining on it directly, the all-pervading heat had found it out: had warmed it almost to the temperature of blood. As the girl drank she saw, out of the corner of her eye, the bush boy settle down beside her. She noticed that he didn't drink from the surface, but reached down, with his fingers outspread, to scoop water from the bottom of the pool. Quick to learn, she too reached down to the rocky bottom. At once the warm surface water was replaced by a current of surprising coolness: a delicious eddy from depths that the rays of the sun had never plumbed. Nectar, with a coolness doubly stimulating: doubly good.

The bush boy drank only a little. Soon he got to his feet, climbed a short way up the cairn, and settled himself on a ledge of rock. Warm in the rays of the setting sun, he watched the strangers with growing curiosity. Not only, he decided, were they freakish in appearance and clumsy in movement, they were also amazingly helpless: untaught, unskilled, utterly incapable of fending for themselves:

perhaps the last survivors of some peculiarly backward tribe. Unless he looked after them, they would die. That was certain. He looked at the children critically; but there was in his appraisal no suggestion of scorn. It was his people's way to accept individuals as they were: to help, not to criticize, the sick, the blind, and the maimed.

He noticed that the smaller of the pair had finished drinking now, and was climbing awkwardly towards him. He leant down, and hauled him on to the ledge of rock.

The water had revived a good deal of Peter's vitality. He was coming now to do something that his sister couldn't bring herself to do: to beg for food. His eyes were on the baby wallaby, still held in the bush boy's hand. He reached out and touched it; tentatively; questioningly.

'Eat?' he said. '*Yeemara?*'

The sun was setting as the boys clambered down from the rock. Twilight, in the Northern Territory, is short. In half an hour it would be quite dark.

The bush boy moved quickly. Skirting the outcrop of rock, he came to a place where a chain of billabongs went looping into the desert: baby poollets, fed from the main pool's overflowing breast. Beside the last of the billabongs was an area of soft sandstone rock: flat, featureless, devoid of vegetation. Here, the bush boy decided, was the site for their fire. He started to clear the area of leaves, twigs, and grass; everything inflammable he swept aside; so that the evil spirits of the bush fire should have nothing to feed on.

Peter watched him. Inquisitive. Imitative. Soon he too started to brush away the leaves and pluck out the blades of grass. And as he worked he fired off questions; his chirpy falsetto echoing shrilly among the rocks.

'What you reckonin' to do, darkie? What you sweepin' the rock like it was a carpet for?'

The bush boy grinned; he'd guessed what the small one wanted to know. On the palm of his hand he placed a dried leaf and a fragment of resin-soaked yacca-yacca; then he

blew on them gently, carefully, as though he were coaxing a
reluctant flame.

'*Larana*,' he said.

'I get it!' Peter was jubilant. 'Fire. You're gonna light a
fire.'

'*Larana*,' the bush boy insisted.

'OK, darkie. *Larana* then. You're gonna light a *Larana*.
I'll help.'

He buckled to; pouncing on bits of debris like a hungry
chicken pecking at scattered corn. The bush boy clicked his
teeth in approval.

From the edge of the pool Mary watched them. Again she
felt a stab of jealousy, mingled this time with envy. She
tried to fight it: told herself it was wrong to feel this way.
But the jealousy wouldn't altogether die. She sensed the
magnetic call of boy to boy: felt left out, alone. If only she
too had been a boy! She lay quietly, face-downward on the
rocks, chin in hands, watching.

Peter followed the bush boy slavishly, copying his every
move. Together, with sharp flints, they scooped a hollow
out of the sandstone: about three feet square and nine
inches deep. Then they started to forage for wood. They
found it in plenty along the fringe of the desert. Yacca-
yaccas: their tall, eight-foot poles, spear-straight, rising
out of the middle of every tuffet of grass. The bush boy
wrenched out the older poles: those that were dry, brittle
with the saplessness of age. Then, amongst the roots, he
fossicked for resin; the exuded sap that had overflowed
from and run down the yacca-yaccas' stems in the days of
their prime. This resin was dry and wax-like: easily
combustible; nature's ready-made firelighter.

Following the bush boy's example; Peter snapped off the
smaller poles, and hunted assiduously for resin.

Then came the snapping of the wood into burnable
fragments, and the grinding of the resin into a gritty pow-
der; then the collecting of stones (not the moisture-
impregnated rock from around the billabongs – which
was liable to explode when heated – but the flat, flinty,

saucer-shaped stones of the desert). And at last the preparations were finished: the fire was ready to be lit.

The bush boy selected a large, smooth-surfaced chip, cut a groove along its centre, then placed it in the hollow in the sandstone. Next he took a slender stem of yacca, and settled the end of it into the groove of the chip. The chip was then covered with wood splinters and sprinkled with powdered resin. Placing an open palm on either side of the yacca stem, the bush boy rubbed his hands together. Slowly at first, then faster and faster, the stem revolved in the groove, creating first friction then heat.

As the sun sank under the rim of the desert, a lazy spiral of wood-smoke rose into the evening air.

The bush boy's hands twisted faster. This was the skill that raised him above the level of the beasts. Bird can call to bird, and animal to animal; mother dingoes can sacrifice themselves for their young; termites can live in highly organized communal towns. But they can't make fire. Man alone can harness the elements.

A blood-red glow suffused the resin. The glow spread; brightened; burst into flame. The boys piled on the sticks of yacca. The fire was made.

The bush boy collected the wallaby; held it by tail-tip over the flames; scorched it down to the bare skin. Then he laid it in the hollow. After a while he picked up a stick and started to lever the fire-heated stones on top of the carcass. Then he banked up the hollow with earth and ash. The rock wallaby baked gently.

An hour later they were eating it, watched by a single dingo and a thin crescent moon. It skinned easily; the flesh was succulent and tender; and there was enough for all.

Before they settled down to sleep the bush boy scattered the fire; stamped out every spark, smoothed out every heap of ash. Then, like a blackstone sentinel, he stood for a while beside the loop of the billabongs, gazing into the desert, interpreting sounds that the children couldn't even hear.

Eventually, satisfied that all was well, he lay down close to the others on the slab of sandstone rock.

A veil of cumulus drifted over the moon.

After a while the dingo crept out of the bush and on to the ledge of sandstone; warily he nosed through the ashes for bones; but he found none. A pair of flying foxes flip-flapped down to the billabong. Little folds of mist moved softly round the hill-that-had-fallen-out-of-the-moon. And the children slept.

ELIZABETH BERRIDGE

Loner

Think of long, hot summer days . . . and the last place you want to be is trapped in an airless classroom, city office or suburban house. So, in your mind, you paint the endless grey streets and buildings outside with the green, red and yellow of living, growing things, and look forward to a weekend trip to the cool, inviting blue of the seaside.

Saturday morning arrives and the whole family rushes to make a quick getaway, but everyone else seems to have had the same idea! You end up squashed in the back of a stuffy car with the seat sticking to your legs and noisy, smelly traffic on all sides. If you had one wish, you'd change into a bird and fly out of the window, over the cars, streets and houses and up into all that blue space.

Unfortunately, some grown-ups have forgotten how to day-dream themselves out of frustrating situations, and so they make the mistake of letting anger get the better of them . . .

Elizabeth Berridge has written this story specially for *Once Upon a Planet*.

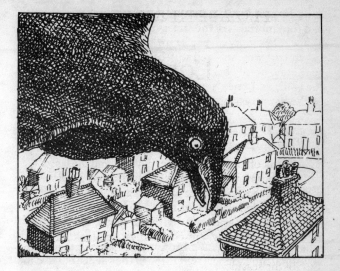

THE SUBURB LAY, LIKE others of its kind, pole-axed under the sun. Its absolute stillness was that of a man hit over the head, stunned, stupefied. It was not so much the silence as the absence of life. In this place everyone held their breath.

It was mid-afternoon. Children still in school and mothers inside the houses, some thinking about what on earth they could give their families for tea. Salad? Weren't they all bored stiff with salads, even if jollied up with tuna fish and cottage cheese? Others lay on their hot beds in curtained rooms, too tired to think about anything but the clogging heat. Fathers were 'in town' behind office windows where square feet of stale air were measured in money.

It had been like this for weeks. The neat gardens were drying up and hose-pipes had been forbidden. From the pavements, across clipped hedges, came the scent of privet and roses and orange blossom. Dicky Tillett, lolling over his desk by the open window in his classroom, took a deep sniff. He could see just beyond the playground over the wall and the emptiness of the streets made him think of a beach at low tide, empty except for rockpools. The trees along the pavements were still and stiff; earlier they had been lopped, so that no untidy branches or fall of leaves would threaten the walkers. Limes, some of them, and they smelt sweetly of the countryside. They dropped sticky syrup on to his father's car, and that annoyed him. Dicky grinned at the memory, although he had had to wash the car clean.

'Wake up, Dicky Tillett! What have I just asked you to do?'

Mr Broome's voice was tired, although he tried to make it brisk and authoritative. The bell would go in a few minutes and then he'd be away; it was far too hot to teach – or to learn.

But before Dicky could gather his wits or understand what his friend was mouthing at him to reply, there came an astonishing sound. It cut through the silence outside the window and the whole class turned its head.

An alien sound echoed across the playground, cutting off the alarm cry of a blackbird. Sharp, derisive, as shocking as a raspberry blown at royalty.

'KAH! Kah! Kah!'

One thought ran, like a perfect experiment in telepathy, through the houses, the gardens, across the streets and through the turned heads of the boys in Mr Broome's class. 'It's laughing at us!'

And again, loud and clear, 'Kah! Kah! Kah!'

There was a rush to the window as the bell rang.

'Hey!' shouted Dicky. 'It's a ruddy great black crow! See? There!'

There it was, landed in the big old horse-chestnut tree in the corner of the playground, looking about it with a bright yellow eye as if amazed at the neat gardens and the alarmed blackbirds and the sycophantic sparrows and the regiments of earthed gnomes condemned to an eternity of fishing in empty concrete pools.

'Kah! Kah! Kah!'

This time the harsh cry was drowned by the ice-cream chimes, like a cheap cinema organ on three notes. The blue and white van, decorated with pictures of cornets and giant ice-lollies, lumbered up to the school gates to wait for its customers.

Dicky's mother, having a quick lie-down at Number 16 Acacia Avenue, started off her bed in a frenzy of mauve nylon ruffles.

'What a cheek, what a row!' Her heart beat lickety-split as she heard the ice-cream chimes joining in and splintering the hot silence of her bedroom. Mauve was a hot colour and nylon was a fabric that refused to breathe. She'd made a mistake there. Poking her face out of the window she spotted the bird flying over the garden. It sat for a moment in the oak tree a few houses away, the sun flashing bright black chips from its sleek back, and its tail feathers moved up perkily.

'You'll get yours,' she informed the bird, as she put on her coolest dress and went downstairs to get tea.

By the time Dicky and his sister Sue came home it had gone, only its mocking shout echoing back from the trees near Bushy Park.

'Did you hear it, Mum?' they asked. 'We saw it at school. What a whopper!'

'It made a right old row. Must be the weather, none of us know where we are in this heat.'

When the children's father came home, hot from his walk up from the station, they told him about it. Frank Tillett was a bird-lover most of the time. He had made a table for them, and regularly put out fat and crumbs in the bad weather.

'Get away,' he said, wanting only to strip off his city clothes and get under the shower. 'Crows live in the country. What would an old crow want here?'

But later, at supper, Dicky couldn't help returning to the subject. The rude cawing, the bright insouciance of the bird, possessed his mind.

'What does it mean, Dad,' he asked, 'straight as the crow

flies? After we'd heard it, Mr Broome told us to find out.'

'Ah.' Frank felt better now. He turned to his son. 'It means that that old blighter can go straight as a die anywhere. He flies in a straight line, nothing to stop him. He could get from here to, say, Box Hill, in ten minutes. Over the trees and away, following his beak. No traffic, see, no roads, no hold-ups.'

'Not like us trying to get to Brighton, Dad,' butted in Sue. 'It took us all day and then we had to have our sandwiches in that stinking old lay-by. Ooh, I wish I was a crow!' and she flapped her arms like wings and sped round the room, calling, 'Caw, caw, caw!' until her parents told her to give over, do.

Frank Tillett tried not to think about the country. He'd been brought up in it, masses of it. It had surrounded him when he was his son's age. The fens lying under that enormous sky, with Ely Cathedral the only real landmark for miles. His uncle had had a farm, and he'd seen crows there. And rooks. Hundreds of rooks, tossed up in the air at sunset like charred paper, calling and settling into the tall elms. Now he said to his children:

'Crows aren't like rooks. Crows are loners.'

'Turned me up,' said his wife. 'I'm glad there's only one.'

'Having a bit of a recce, that's what it was doing. Gone back to where it came from, I expect.'

'D'you remember that fox I saw in the spring, Dad? Jumping over the fence by the shed – early in the morning?'

'You put out that chicken carcass for it, got it out of the dustbin,' accused his mother. 'Nasty dirty thing, encouraging it.'

'It wasn't dirty! It was beautiful! It had a great bushy red tail –'

'Well, we don't want wild animals round here. Those hedgehogs were bad enough. Full of fleas.'

It was no use arguing with his mother, Dicky knew. She

wouldn't even let him have a dog or a cat. They'd get under her feet, and who'd clear up after them? She'd give him urban foxes! They were all right on the telly, but not in her garden, thank you.

But, in spite of their mother, the children knew that small wild things did live in their neat garden, hiding out of sight. The two toads, for instance, who lurked in the rockery near the bird-bath. On the hot day the ants had swarmed, they had ventured out on to the lawn in the middle of the afternoon, crawling about and darting out their long tongues to feast on the winged ants that fell to the ground after their nuptial flight was over. Dicky and Sue had put down a shallow dish of water and watched them sprawl in it, with great grins of pleasure at the coolness. And on a small clump of nettles, in the tiny corner the children had for their own, there were a few Small Tortoiseshell caterpillars. There were a pair of grey squirrels, too, who lived in the oak tree and robbed the bird-table as well as frisking down for their own food. 'Fair's fair,' their father had said, putting out nuts.

But all these creatures came and went at their own will, and sometimes Dicky wished he belonged to a quite different ent family, like Gerald Durrell's, living in Greece and having all those animals and insects and birds to care for as pets. Fancy keeping a scorpion in a matchbox! Barn owls, magpies, lizards, fish – what a lucky devil! And nobody seemed to mind. Once, when Dicky was much younger, he had kept an ant in a matchbox and spent hours examining it through his mother's magnifying glass. Then it had changed into a monster, covered with fine hairs, looking at him with great eyes and moving its jaws hungrily when he fed it grains of sugar. It had legs with bristles and hooks and appeared to comb itself when it had eaten, he could swear. He had taken it to school when his teacher had asked the children to bring their pets. Other boys and girls had brought golden hamsters and mice and guinea-pigs. One boy had stick insects and you could hardly pick them out from the twigs they balanced on. Dicky was the only one to bring an ant, and somebody had trodden on it when it scuttled out of the matchbox. They'd all laughed.

The next day the crow was back, sailing over the streets and houses, giving its derisive call. At tea-time it pecked at the cherries in the next-door garden and then was off again, its mocking voice forming a wake of noise, floating and sinking like the tail of a paper kite.

'It gets on my nerves, Frank. I could swear it's laughing at us.'

'Well, we can't help living here. Not when I have to get to the bank –'

His wife looked at him in astonishment.

'What are you on about? We *chose* to live here. We like it, what's wrong with Giggs Green?'

Frank couldn't really say, but he felt uneasy and resentful. All that weekend the crow came over, twice a day, and he had to put up with his wife's complaints. Then he made up his mind. He looked out his airgun, one he'd kept since he was a boy. He'd been a fair shot, picking off the odd rabbit or pigeon. He was keeping the gun for his son, when he was of an age, looking forward to taking him out into the country – they'd go back to Cambridgeshire, see if his uncle was still alive, teach Dicky how to use it.

The heat sharpened his temper. The lawn grew browner under the unremitting sun. Even bowls of washing-up water didn't do much for it, and he dared not use the hose, for fear of nosy neighbours. He was a careful man, Frank Tillett, oiling and sharpening the dozen or so implements he needed to keep his garden in check. But sometimes he longed for the real country; a deep green wood, a liquid stream. He'd like to take the whole family out into that real country – but not if it meant sitting in traffic jams. That old crow could go there, straight as a die, any time he chose. A bitter envy settled on Frank as heavily and blackly as the bird itself settled into the trees around Acacia Avenue. The next-door neighbour didn't mind it tearing away at his cherries; for what the crow didn't eat, starlings and black-birds did. When he saw Frank cleaning his gun, he said, shocked, 'Oh, fair play, Frank, if we don't mind him having the cherries, why should you? Anyway, it's not allowed by law, is it? Shooting in a built-up area?'

Frank was evasive. 'Oh,' he said, smoothing oil where it was needed, 'just scare the blighter, like. I'm used to birds. Born in the country, wasn't I?'

'Birds should know their place,' he said to the family over supper. 'Ungrateful, that's what they are. Feed 'em through the winter and in the spring they tear your crocuses to bits and in the summer they eat your strawberries, and –'

'I like birds,' said Sue. 'I don't mind them eating our stuff. We've got plenty.'

'We're reading about jackdaws and ravens at school,' said Dicky. 'Mr Broome's got a book called *King Solomon's Ring*. The man who wrote it lived in Germany and tamed all kinds of birds. He could talk to them. He had a cockatoo once and it bit off all the buttons on his father's jacket and trousers while he was asleep.'

'Buttons on trousers?' exclaimed his mother. 'It's all zips now. That's nice, I must say!'

The children were still asleep when Frank got up the next morning at five. There was something private and pearly about this untouched time of day, even in the suburbs. He heard the dawn chorus from the paved terrace, holding the gun over his knee, and watched the day break cleanly, like a great egg, and the sun come flooding out over the mysterious milky sky. Ruddy marvellous, made you think. Made you remember mornings in childhood – the cold dawn over the fens, the space, the land and sky empty and waiting. He wanted his children to have such a childhood. His anger, which had been seething for a week, like porridge, subsided. What had he got up for?

Then he heard it, coming straight over.

'Kah! Kah! Kah!'

It was a black blot on that pure sky. He sat quite still, edging his gun on to his shoulder, sighting along the barrel.

'Kah! Kah! Kah!'

It had never come so close. It was bending the branches of

the laburnum near the trellis, sitting there with its bright despising eyes full on the prisoner of Number 16. A quick dekko at all you lot in this built-up area and I'm off, straight as the crow flies, that's me. I'll be in Ely by tea-time.

'Oh no,' whispered Frank Tillett, 'not this time, mate.'

He fired.

The bird seemed to spin and stagger. Then it flapped from the tree to the trellis, its claws trying to clutch a hold, but its wings weighed it down. Clumsily it flopped, a thrown-out rag, on to the terrace at Frank's feet.

Above his head a window was flung open and his wife's shriek broke his concentration. As he lowered the gun, Dicky came running out of the back door, holding up his pyjamas and crying.

'I've winged it, great black booby,' said his father flatly. 'Ought to finish it off.' But he stood there, just looking.

'Don't finish him off, Dad, don't!'

Frank watched his son bending over it. He thought he detected a dying out of hostility in the bird's bright eye. It opened its beak but no sound came. Dicky put a hand on the bird's wing and the yellow beak came swiftly round to peck at him.

'I can mend his wing. I can. I can have him as a pet. Let me keep it, Dad, and I'll put it in the shed and then it won't be all over the house, like cats and dogs, and Mum can't . . .' Dicky didn't know how he could mend its wing, nor what he was saying. But he kept himself between his parents and the crippled bird, wiping his tears away with his fist. To his surprise, his father said not one word, only went indoors and straight upstairs to the bathroom.

People were looking out of their windows. Who was shooting? Was it terrorists?

Dicky went to school with Sue. Neither of them had eaten any breakfast, and when, in the afternoon, Mr Broome said jokingly that the crow must have found a better place to go to, he put his hand up and asked to be excused. He ran straight home.

The crow had dragged itself under the cotoneaster by the

wall. It lay there, on its side, its feet twitching. It was alive. Dicky brought it a dish of bread and milk. He found a worm, but it didn't eat it. Its injured wing was bent at an awkward angle, but it wasn't severed. When Dicky's father came home, the children begged him to take it to the vet.

Frank Tillett had had a wretched day. He'd been brought up to make a clean kill, his uncle had insisted on it. But he couldn't bring himself to shoot the crow, on the ground and in front of his family. His wife said nothing, kept her distance. So, without a word, he found a cardboard box and Dicky lifted the bird in. In silence he drove with his children to the nearest vet.

The vet was an elderly man, a mild man, but he frowned when Frank told him what had happened. He mentioned the police. Then he said that he wasn't used to handling wild birds, but as there was no wild-bird sanctuary near, he'd do his best. Very gently he tried to flex the wings, avoiding the searching beak.

'We'll have a go. It's shock, really, that kills a wild bird – the smaller kind, that is. Now we're in luck. Just watch. This wing isn't broken, it's dislocated, and I think –' As the children watched, enthralled, his clever fingers probed and manipulated. There was a faint click and the wing straightened. 'Good. Now the flight feathers have been damaged by the pellets, and I'll have to extract what I can.' He worked on. 'Mind you, this chap'll need some care, but he's a young bird . . .'

'What shall we do?' asked Dicky.

'We'll make him a cage out of that packing case we've got in the shed. I'll put a wire front in,' said his father. 'Right, what about food? You two will have to look after it, mind.'

'Oh, we will,' cried Sue. 'Won't we, Dicky?'

'Minced worms mixed with raw egg. Leather-jackets, if you can get them. Don't forget that crows are called the farmer's friends. It'll eat anything, really, fruit. Now you might have to put the first lot down its beak, if you hold it like this –'

He showed them and to their surprise the crow did not

try to attack him. 'You can let it go free when its feathers have grown.' He put a hand on Dicky's shoulder. 'Now, let me know how he goes on. And, Mr Tillett, I shouldn't try shooting any more birds, if I were you.'

Frank felt a real fool, but he was man enough to say that he was sorry, he didn't know what had got into him. That evening, as he worked on the packing case, Dicky put a hand on his arm and said, 'Never mind, Dad, we'll tame him, you'll see. You've made a super cage. We'll call him Korky, because that's the sound he makes, and it's like Korky the cat – the one in the comic strip. And Mr Broome'll look things up in that book.' He felt sorry for his father, and didn't want him to go on feeling bad.

As the days went by, the crow never worried Mrs Tillett. It sat hunched in the packing case, moving its wings about, walking to the front of the cage and pecking at the wire. It didn't make a sound, but you wouldn't call it tame, not with that look in its eye.

'Maybe you should have finished it off, Frank,' she said. 'It gives me such a funny look when I go down to hang out the washing.'

'But he's eating, Mum. He knows his name. Korky.'

Sue was good with him. She managed to push the first lot of food down his beak – a gooey mess of minced worms and raw egg and breadcrumbs – while Dicky held it open. Gradually he began to eat by himself and looked out for them, giving a low caw as they came down the garden with a dish of food, and a dish of water. Mr Broome got the boys and girls to collect leather-jackets and worms, and came to see him. He took Frank off to the pub for a drink, and they became quite good friends. But the crow never took to Frank. He seemed to know, somehow. Whenever he came near, he would lower his head and make a rattle in his throat, and quiver his wings.

When the vet came round he, too, was pleased.

'Look,' he said, 'the feathers are growing and he looks quite glossy. He'll soon be able to fly properly. Let's open the cage door and see what he does.'

At first the crow walked out of the shed, looking about him. Then he hopped a few feet, flapped his wings. Dicky and Sue were hunkered down on the grass, watching intently. Suddenly he gave a jump and landed on Dicky's arm.

'Hold still,' said the vet softly. 'See what he does.'

The crow inched up Dicky's arm, poked gently at his ear, then pulled his hair. He said, quite distinctly, 'Kor-ky, Kor-ky.'

Dicky went bright red. He wasn't scared, but that beak was very near his cheek. His arm ached through keeping it so still. But the bird had spoken, didn't everyone realize that? He had said his name!

'Jump off, Korky,' said Dicky. 'Jump off. Here's some of Mum's fruit cake.'

At once Korky jumped off and looked for the cake, ate it, and walked back to the shed, had a drink of water, stood inside his cage.

'Clever little devil,' exclaimed the vet. 'He knows it's not quite time to go.'

That night the weather broke. The glorious refreshing rain came pouring down. And that night, too, the family had an argument. Dicky and Sue were sure the crow had spoken his name. Their parents said he was just trying out his caw. Sue, to the annoyance of her mother, went flying round the room again, calling 'Kor-ky, Kor-ky . . .'

'I hope it's not going to sit in that shed all the winter,' said Mrs Tillett. She was the only member of the family to call Korky 'it' instead of 'he'.

'We'll leave the door open and pull back the wire from the front of the packing case,' said Frank. 'Then he can please himself.'

A few days after that, when they went to feed him, the shed was empty.

'Oh,' wailed Sue. 'He's gone!'

Dicky felt a lump in his throat. 'We'll leave his food, just in case.'

They walked back up the garden, and from the kitchen window their mother watched them. Something must have happened, she knew, they looked so dejected. Then she saw a black object hurtle down from the cherry tree and land on her son's shoulder. She heard the sound she had so hated. But somehow — wasn't it different? The cawing had no mocking tone, it sounded more like a greeting. To her horror, she saw the bird pecking at Dicky's hair, and ran out, flapping her hands. At once it flew off, but only to the fence.

'That's all we need,' she scolded, 'a tame crow that pecks out people's eyes!'

'They don't peck out people's eyes, Mum. There's an old German proverb that says that one crow won't peck out the eye of another —'

'Since when have you been a crow?'

'. . . And a tame crow or raven won't peck out the eye of a human being. It's in —'

'Mr Broome's book! I'll have to buy that book to see for myself,' said his mother.

'I'll keep you to that! Hey, Sue, what are you doing?'

Sue was running into the kitchen, and she came back with something in her hand. 'Why didn't he come to *me*?' she said crossly. 'I've fed him and fed him and minced up hundreds of worms — I think he's ungrateful!'

'Maybe you're too little,' said her mother.

'Maybe he thinks you're frightened,' said Dicky.

At once she held out her hand with a slice of cake in it.

'I'm not frightened. Look. Come on, Korky, here's a slice of Mum's fruit cake —'

'So that's where my cake goes,' grumbled Mrs Tillett, but she couldn't help smiling. 'Wasting my good cake on an old crow —'

Korky flew on to Sue's wrist and pecked at the cake. But he couldn't balance properly, and walked up to her elbow. His claws tickled, but she said nothing.

'You'd better get off to school. Say goodbye to that bird, it's given us enough trouble.'

At dinner-time, when everybody was in the playground, they heard a sound they had nearly forgotten.

'Kah! Kah! Kah-keey!'

But this time the black shape encircled the building, as if looking for something – or someone. It checked its flight, planed down and landed in the horse-chestnut tree, looking about with bright eyes, its tail feather perked up.

Mr Broome came over to Dicky and Sue. 'I don't expect he'll come down, there are too many people here,' he said. 'My, isn't he handsome?'

'D'you think he'll stay? I can't bear to see him go,' said Dicky. 'But it'll be awkward.'

'He'll find a mate, I expect,' said Mr Broome. 'He'll be off to his old haunts, which is how it should be. But I'll be a Dutchman if he doesn't come visiting.'

Mr Broome didn't turn into a Dutchman, for one day, just before the start of the autumn term, there were two black blobs high up in the sky, circling and calling. Korky and his mate sat in the oak tree near the children's garden and watched. But they did not venture any nearer.

'I know why,' said Dicky. 'Korky hasn't forgotten what happened. They're intelligent, crows.'

When they were gone, Sue said, 'I'm glad we didn't tame him, aren't you?'

'I suppose so,' said Dicky slowly. 'But he did know his name. That wasn't an ordinary caw, you know. It was Kor-ky, or Kah-key . . .'

'Well, I wouldn't want to be tamed if I was a crow,' said Sue. 'I'd never come near the human race. I'd live near Ely, like Dad did, and fly over the fens and be safe.'

'But the best thing,' said Dicky thoughtfully, 'was that we made friends with a wild bird. That's brill. And when I grow up –'

But he retreated into one of his long silences, and Sue knew better than to wait for him to finish. Instead she wandered off to find a piece of fruit cake. Now that Korky had gone, she could be sure that there would be some left.

BARBARA SMUCKER

Amish Adventure

The Amish community of North America still live today as they did in the last century. They do not believe that people should strive for riches and power over each other and the Earth, for our selfishness and greed can upset the balance of Nature, endangering the planet and everything on it. And so they take just enough from the land for their real needs: food, shelter and warmth, but no more. They work together, helping each other in all things and sharing their few possessions. They refuse to fight or defend themselves, knowing that violence breeds violence. Their patient old world, re-assuring, quiet and peaceful, is surrounded on all sides by a reckless young world that is confusing, lonely, loud and exciting.

It is almost as if young Ian McDonald has gone back in time: one minute he is being driven to his Aunt Clem's by Jack Trent, an acquaintance of his father, the next minute, their speeding car crashes headlong into an Amish buggy. The horse, Star, dies instantly; its owner, Ezra Bender, is badly injured. Jack Trent is taken away in shock, and the Bender family look after Ian on their Amish farm. Suddenly, Ian finds himself with a foot in each world . . .

IAN'S PROBLEMS SEEMED to pile higher and higher into a tottering heap. Always before he could tell them to his dad, the two of them had worried together about the solutions. But his father was miles away and it might take weeks for letters to travel to and from the Northwest Territories. He had the oil company's phone number, but Dad might not be available. There was no phone at the Benders for Dad to call back and anyway he wasn't yet sure what he wanted to say.

He couldn't ignore Aunt Clem much longer. She was a determined woman. She expected him for the winter and she didn't change plans abruptly. What would she think of this farm where he wanted to stay? 'No electricity! No inside bathroom! No rugs! No curtains! No automobile! It's not civilized! . . .' He could just hear her.

The fantasy of believing he could escape backwards in time was totally banished every time he stood on the slope of ground that led to the second floor of the barn. He could see cars in the distance speeding one after another along a busy, modern highway.

Jonah appeared at his side, tapping with his cane.

'We're ploughing one of the fields this afternoon for winter wheat, Ian,' he said. 'Reuben is going to use the one-furrow plough. You walk behind it with him and watch. If you could stay with us for a time, you might be able to help plough the corn fields next month.'

'If you could stay with us . . .' Ian repeated Jonah's words over and over to himself. Jonah had said it four times now. He must really mean it. Maybe he wasn't joking about learning to plough?

Jonah stood squarely in front of him. His wide chest pulled at the buttons of his home-made shirt with each deep breath, and the flowing white beard moved up and down. Jonah's sharp blue eyes, half-closed with tiredness, looked directly into Ian's. There was a mixture of laughter and approval in them.

'I can see you don't give up easily, Ian,' he said.

'I'll find Reuben right away.' Ian ran through the large barn door to the stalls where Reuben was throwing a harness over a huge dapple-grey horse.

'Hi, Reuben.' Ian was breathless. 'Jonah said you'd show me how to plough and how to harness a horse.'

'Sure, Ian.' Reuben smoothed the horse's sides with both hands. 'Dick here is a Percheron Gelding. See his big strong feet and look how broad he is across the chest. I like him best, next to Star. He has an honest face and he'll do anything for Poppa and me.'

Reuben put his thumb into the side of big Dick's mouth, slipping a steel bit into an open space between his teeth. Ian shuddered. Could he do this? Wouldn't the horse bite with those sharp, white teeth? Then Ian looked at Dick's gentle, placid brown eyes. If Reuben could stick his finger inside Dick's mouth, he could too.

'Help me get the bridle behind his ears,' Reuben said. Ian slipped the leather strap behind the two stiff, pointed ears.

'Giddyup,' Reuben called out to Dick.

'Giddyup,' Ian shouted as loudly as he could.

The horse backed up obediently from his stall.

Outside, Dick was hooked up to a small plough. Reuben grabbed both handles and also held a single line from the horse in his right hand.

'If I yell "Gee", he'll go right. If I yell "Haw", he goes left,' Reuben explained. 'Now watch, Ian. I have to plough a straight furrow.' Reuben pointed across the huge flat field in front of them. 'I keep my eye on that white cloth tied to the fence way over there. It keeps me going straight.'

Reuben flicked the line. Dick strained forward with his wide shoulders. The plough cut into the black earth, folding it back in ripples. On the far side of the same field another farmer ploughed with a five-horse hitch. The strong animals bent their heads together as though marching to beating drums in a parade. Their flowing manes streamed out like flags in the wind.

'When you see any rocks, Ian, throw them in a pile between the furrows,' Reuben called loudly.

The stones spilled out round and hard from the upturned soil. Ian hoped he could do this rock-throwing job. It took a lot of strength.

After an exhausting half-hour, Jonah hobbled to Ian's side and both of them watched a beardless farmer across the road bouncing comfortably on the seat of a new red tractor. He ploughed swiftly over his fields, taking half the time of the horse-drawn ploughs.

'Why don't you have a tractor?' Ian asked somewhat enviously.

'Yah well,' Jonah said. 'If people let all these new contraptions do their work for them, they won't have enough work to keep them busy and safe from trouble. And besides,' the old man went on with a chuckle in his voice, 'a horse reproduces; a tractor produces nothing but debts.'

Ian wasn't convinced. 'That doesn't sound like a good enough reason.'

'Yah well,' Jonah went on, 'our neighbour across the road does things differently. He plants just one crop to make money and his soil wears out growing the same thing year after year – even with chemical fertilizer. What we do is rotate our crops and plough manure from our own barn into the soil. That way the land is enriched and more can be raised on less land.'

Jonah left to go back to the barn as Reuben came towards them, swinging the plough into an arc at the end of another row.

'My turn,' said Ian, grabbing the handles of the plough away from Reuben in his eagerness. Reuben hesitated. 'Giddyup,' Ian cried, wanting to speed up the ploughing and not to be totally outstripped by the racing tractor. Dick gave a quick tug and the blades of the hand-plough left the furrow and bounced along over the surface of the field. Dick changed his course and headed for the bush and a lush patch of tall green grass. Ian clung to the handles with all of his strength. The great horse raised his head and shook it free of the restraining line. Then he peacefully lowered his mouth and began to nibble. Ian was sure that he saw a grin on Dick's face.

'Now, what did I do wrong?' Ian stomped up to the animal, his face crimson with indignation. The horse looked at him with feigned innocence.

Reuben bent over laughing. 'You look like your head is on fire. You want to learn everything too fast, Ian. Dick doesn't know you and I still have to show you how to hold the handles.'

Ian sank to the ground beside Dick. Couldn't he ever do one of these jobs right? His arms ached, his feet hurt and sprays of pain shot through his back each time he bent it. How could he help the Benders if he blundered around like this?

Ian stretched out on the green grass. Dick's sharp, white teeth chomped beside him. He was surprised to discover that he wasn't afraid. He was determined that he and Dick were going to learn to work together. You couldn't feel this way about a tractor, and he'd have to admit this to Jonah.

For the next hour, however, he left the ploughing to

Reuben, and consoled himself by piling up as many stones as he could. Eventually Rebecca appeared swinging a bucket of cold lemonade and some tin cups.

'Thirsty, Ian?' she asked and handed him one of the cups. He drank it in two swallows. Rebecca smiled at him warmly.

Reuben ploughed one last furrow before they started back to the barn. As they neared it, Ian saw the back of a police car disappearing down the lane. Grossdoddy Jonah stood in a swirl of dust behind it.

'We've finished,' Reuben called out and walked off alone to unharness Dick in the barn. A little spiral of fear uncoiled inside Ian, for Jonah seemed to hesitate on the lane as though wanting to postpone his return to the farmhouse. He leaned so heavily on his cane that the end of it tunnelled into the ground. The clear blue of his eyes seemed clouded. A hazy glow of amber spread behind Jonah from the setting sun, like the dying embers of a camp fire. The muted light illuminated his beard and his white bobbed hair, so that they became startling puffs of luminous clouds. He didn't seem real.

'Ach, Ian.' Jonah broke the spell of Indian summer. 'The news is not good about Ezra. The leg had to come off in the operation. He must stay in the hospital for some time. The other leg is partially paralysed. He may never walk again.'

Ian stood in mute shock. What would the Benders do? How could a man who might never walk again work on an Amish farm? Ian would *have* to stay and help the family now, even with all the blunders he made. And where was John? If he knew about his father, surely John would sell his car and come home? But if John didn't come back, even Aunt Clem might see why Ian had to stay. He forced himself to ask Jonah about her.

'Ach yah, I forgot.' Jonah straightened his back and began walking to the farmhouse. Ian saw the shaft he had cracked leaning in two pieces against the barn. It was an embarrassment just to look at them. Jonah didn't notice.

'Your aunt is better,' Jonah said. 'She is coming for you soon. She doesn't like it that you are staying on an Amish farm.'

RUDYARD KIPLING

How Fear Came

from *The Jungle Book*

The jungle is a place where life seems to have exploded into millions of different living things; a place where as much wildlife as lives in a whole city is found in a patch of jungle the size of a garden. No wonder tropical rainforest explorers tell of how it *really* hums with activity.

But the rainforest is not just a group of creatures that happen to have moved into the same neighbourhood and are all 'doing their own thing'. It is like a living house of cards. Imagine a great pile of playing cards, each decorated with one jungle plant or animal. One by one, day by day, the colourful cards are balanced delicately against each other. After millions of years and with infinite patience, a vast and beautiful palace is built. The jungle is like that card palace. If you take away one card from the towering turrets on top, by killing all the rainforest gorillas, for example, many other cards and creatures begin to fall. If you take away a card from the very bottom, perhaps the tall jungle trees themselves, then the whole great palace tumbles down for ever. For with the trees gone, the thin soil is washed away by wind and rain . . . All living things on our planet are in delicate balance, like the jungle and that 'house of cards'.

Rudyard Kipling gives the flavour of a real Indian jungle, together with the excitement of a good story. When the jungle animals speak, they do so as creatures of the wild, never becoming too human. Mowgli is a 'man-cub' who has grown up with a family of wolves. In this story, all the animals face one terrible danger . . .

The stream is shrunk – the pool is dry,
And we be comrades, thou and I;
With fevered jowl and dusty flank
Each jostling each along the bank;
And by one drouthy fear made still,
Forgoing thought of quest or kill.
Now 'neath his dam the fawn may see
The lean Pack-wolf as cowed as he,
And the tall buck, unflinching, note
The fangs that tore his father's throat.
The pools are shrunk – the streams are dry
And we be playmates, thou and I,
Till yonder cloud – Good Hunting! – loose
The rain that breaks our Water Truce.

THE LAW OF THE JUNGLE – which is by far the oldest law in the world – has arranged for almost every kind of accident that may befall the Jungle-People, till now its code is as perfect as time and custom can make it. You will remember that Mowgli spent a great part of his life in the Seeonee Wolf-Pack, learning the Law from Baloo, the Brown Bear; and it was Baloo who told him, when the boy grew impatient at the constant orders, that the Law was like the Giant Creeper, because it dropped across everyone's back and no one could escape. 'When thou hast lived as long as I have, Little Brother, thou wilt see how all the Jungle obeys at least one Law. And that will be no pleasant sight,' said Baloo.

This talk went in at one ear and out at the other, for a boy who spends his life eating and sleeping does not worry about anything till it actually stares him in the face. But, one year, Baloo's words came true, and Mowgli saw all the Jungle working under the Law.

It began when the winter Rains failed almost entirely, and Ikki, the Porcupine, meeting Mowgli in a bamboo-thicket, told him that the wild yams were drying up. Now everybody knows that Ikki is ridiculously fastidious in his choice of food, and will eat nothing but the very best and ripest. So Mowgli laughed and said, 'What is that to me?'

'Not much *now*,' said Ikki, rattling his quills in a stiff, uncomfortable way, 'but later we shall see. Is there any more diving into the deep rock-pool below the Bee-Rocks, Little Brother?'

'No. The foolish water is going all away, and I do not wish to break my head,' said Mowgli, who, in those days, was quite sure that he knew as much as any five of the Jungle-People put together.

'That is thy loss. A small crack might let in some wisdom.' Ikki ducked quickly to prevent Mowgli from pulling his nose-bristles, and Mowgli told Baloo what Ikki had said. Baloo looked very grave, and mumbled half to himself: 'If I were alone I would change my hunting-grounds now, before the others began to think. And yet – hunting among strangers ends in fighting, and they might hurt the Man-cub. We must wait and see how the *mohwa* blooms.'

That spring the *mohwa* tree, that Baloo was so fond of, never flowered. The greeny, cream coloured, waxy blossoms were heat-killed before they were born, and only a few bad-smelling petals came down when he stood on his hind legs and shook the tree. Then, inch by inch, the untempered heat crept into the heart of the Jungle, turning it yellow, brown, and at last black. The green growths in the sides of the ravines burned up to broken wires and curled films of dead stuff; the hidden pools sank down and caked over, keeping the last least footmark on their edges as if it had been cast in iron; the juicy-stemmed creepers fell away from the trees they clung to and died at their feet; the bamboos withered, clanking when the hot winds blew, and the moss peeled off the rocks deep in the Jungle, till they were as bare and as hot as the quivering blue boulders in the bed of the stream.

The birds and the Monkey-People went north early in the year, for they knew what was coming; and the deer and the wild pig broke far away to the perished fields of the villages, dying sometimes before the eyes of men too weak to kill them. Chil, the Kite, stayed and grew fat, for there was a great deal of carrion, and evening after evening he brought the news to the beasts, too weak to force their way to fresh hunting-grounds that the sun was killing the Jungle for three days' flight in every direction.

Mowgli, who had never known what real hunger meant, fell back on stale honey, three years old, scraped out of deserted rock-hives – honey black as a sloe, and dusty with dried sugar. He hunted, too, for deep-boring grubs under the bark of the trees, and robbed the wasps of their new broods. All the game in the Jungle was no more than skin and bone, and Bagheera could kill thrice in a night, and hardly get a full meal. But the want of water was the worst, for though the Jungle-People drink seldom they must drink deep.

And the heat went on and on, and sucked up all the moisture, till at last the main channel of the Waingunga was the only stream that carried a trickle of water between its dead banks; and when Hathi, the Wild Elephant, who lives for a hundred years and more, saw a long, lean blue ridge of rock show dry in the very centre of the stream, he knew that he was looking at the Peace Rock, and then and there he lifted up his trunk and proclaimed the Water Truce, as his father before him had proclaimed it fifty years ago. The deer, wild pig, and buffalo took up the cry hoarsely; and Chil, the Kite, flew in great circles far and wide, whistling and shrieking the warning.

By the Law of the Jungle it is death to kill at the drinking-places when once the Water Truce has been declared. The reason of this is that drinking comes before eating. Every one in the Jungle can scramble along somehow when only game is scarce; but water is water, and when there is but one source of supply, all hunting stops while the Jungle-People go there for their needs. In good seasons, when water was plentiful, those who came down to drink at the Waingunga – or anywhere else, for that matter – did so at the risk of their lives, and that risk made no small part of the fascination of the night's doings. To move down so cunningly that never a leaf stirred; to wade knee-deep in the roaring shallows that drown all noise from behind; to drink, looking backward over one shoulder, every muscle ready for the first desperate bound of keen terror; to roll on the sandy margin, and return, wet-muzzled and well plumped out, to the admiring herd, was a thing that all tall-antlered young bucks took a delight in, precisely because they knew that at any moment Bagheera or Shere Khan might leap upon them and bear them down. But now all that life-and-death fun was ended, and the Jungle-People came up, starved and weary, to the shrunken river – tiger, bear, deer, buffalo, and pig, all together – drank the fouled waters, and hung above them, too exhausted to move off.

The deer and the pig had tramped all day in search of something better than dried bark and withered leaves. The buffaloes had found no wallows to be cool in, and no green crops to steal. The snakes had left the Jungle and come down to the river in the hope of finding a stray frog. They curled round wet stones, and never offered to strike when the nose of a rooting pig dislodged them. The river-turtles had long ago been killed by Bagheera, cleverest of hunters, and the fish had buried themselves deep in the dry mud.

Only the Peace Rock lay across the shallows like a long snake, and the little tired ripples hissed as they dried on its hot side.

It was here that Mowgli came nightly for the cool and the companionship. The most hungry of his enemies would hardly have cared for the boy then. His naked hide made him seem more lean and wretched than any of his fellows. His hair was bleached to tow colour by the sun; his ribs stood out like the ribs of a basket, and the lumps on his knees and elbows, where he was used to track on all fours, gave his shrunken limbs the look of knotted grass-stems. But his eye, under his matted forelock, was cool and quiet, for Bagheera was his adviser in this time of trouble, and told him to go quietly, hunt slowly, and never, on any account, to lose his temper.

'It is an evil time,' said the Black Panther, one furnace-hot evening, 'but it will go if we can live till the end. Is thy stomach full, Man-cub?'

'There is stuff in my stomach, but I get no good of it. Think you, Bagheera, the Rains have forgotten us and will never come again?'

'Not I! We shall see the *mohwa* in blossom yet, and the little fawns all fat with new grass. Come down to the Peace Rock and hear the news. On my back, Little Brother.'

'This is no time to carry weight. I can still stand alone, but – indeed we be no fatted bullocks, we two.'

Bagheera looked along his ragged, dusty flank and whispered: 'Last night I killed a bullock under the yoke. So low was I brought that I think I should not have dared to spring if he had been loose. *Wou!*'

Mowgli laughed. 'Yes, we be great hunters now,' said he. 'I am very bold – to eat grubs,' and the two came down together through the crackling undergrowth to the river-bank and the lacework of shoals that ran out from it in every direction.

'The water cannot live long,' said Baloo, joining them. 'Look across. Yonder are trails like the roads of Man.'

On the level plain of the farther bank the stiff jungle-grass had died standing, and, dying, had mummied. The beaten tracks of the deer and the pig, all heading toward the river, had striped that colourless plain with dusty gullies driven through the ten-foot grass, and, early as it was, each long avenue was full of first-comers hastening to the water. You could hear the does and fawns coughing in the snuff-like dust.

Upstream, at the bend of the sluggish pool round the Peace Rock, and Warden of the Water Truce, stood Hathi, the Wild Elephant, with his sons, gaunt and grey in the moonlight, rocking to and fro – always rocking. Below him a little were the vanguard of the deer; below these, again, the pig and the wild buffalo; and on the opposite bank, where the tall trees came down to the water's edge, was the place set apart for the Eaters of Flesh – the tiger, the wolves, the panther, the bear, and the others.

'We are under one Law, indeed,' said Bagheera, wading into the water and looking across at the lines of clicking horns and starting eyes where the deer and the pig pushed each other to and fro. 'Good hunting, all you of my blood,' he added, lying down at full length, one flank thrust out of the shallows; and then, between his teeth, 'But for that which is the Law it would be *very* good hunting.'

The quick-spread ears of the deer caught the last sentence, and a frightened whisper ran along the ranks. 'The Truce! Remember the Truce!'

'Peace there, peace!' gurgled Hathi, the Wild Elephant. 'The Truce holds, Bagheera. This is no time to talk of hunting.'

'Who should know better than I?' Bagheera answered, rolling his yellow eyes upstream. 'I am an eater of turtles – a fisher of frogs. *Ngaayah!* Would I could get good from chewing branches!'

'*We* wish so, very greatly,' bleated a young fawn, who had only been born that spring, and did not at all like it. Wretched as the Jungle People were, even Hathi could not help chuckling; while Mowgli, lying on his elbows in the warm water, laughed aloud, and beat up the scum with his feet.

'Well spoken, little bud-horn,' Bagheera purred. 'When the Truce ends that shall be remembered in thy favour,' and he looked keenly through the darkness to make sure of recognizing the fawn again.

Gradually the talking spread up and down the drinking-places. One could hear the scuffling, snorting pig asking for more room; the buffaloes grunting among themselves as they lurched out across the sand-bars, and the deer telling pitiful stories of their long footsore wanderings in quest of food. Now and again they asked some question of the Eaters of Flesh across the river, but all the news was bad, and the roaring hot wind of the Jungle came and went between the rocks and the rattling branches, and scattered twigs and dust on the water.

'The men-folk, too, they die beside their ploughs,' said a young sambhur. 'I passed three between sunset and night. They lay still, and their bullocks with them. We also shall lie still in a little.'

'The river has fallen since last night,' said Baloo. 'O Hathi, hast thou ever seen the like of this drought?'

'It will pass, it will pass,' said Hathi, squirting water along his back and sides.

'We have one here that cannot endure long,' said Baloo; and he looked towards the boy he loved.

'I?' said Mowgli indignantly, sitting up in the water. 'I have no long fur to cover my bones, but – but if *thy* hide were taken off, Baloo –'

Hathi shook all over at the idea, and Baloo said severely:

'Man-Cub, that is not seemly to tell a Teacher of the Law. *Never* have I been seen without my hide.'

'Nay, I meant no harm, Baloo; but only that thou art, as it were, like the coconut in the husk, and I am the same coconut all naked. Now that brown husk of thine –' Mowgli was sitting cross-legged, and explaining things with his forefinger in his usual way, when Bagheera put out a paddy paw and pulled him over backward into the water.

'Worse and worse,' said the Black Panther, as the boy rose spluttering. 'First Baloo is to be skinned, and now he is a coconut. Be careful that he does not do what the ripe coconuts do.'

'And what is that?' said Mowgli, off his guard for the minute, though that is one of the oldest catches in the Jungle.

'Break thy head,' said Bagheera quietly, pulling him under again.

'It is not good to make a jest of thy teacher,' said the bear, when Mowgli had been ducked for the third time.

'Not good! What would ye have? That naked thing running to and fro makes a monkey-jest of those who have once been good hunters, and pulls the best of us by the whiskers for sport.' This was Shere Khan, the Lame Tiger, limping down to the water. He waited a little to enjoy the sensation he made among the deer on the opposite bank; then he dropped his square, frilled head and began to lap, growling: 'The Jungle has become a whelping-ground for naked cubs, now. Look at me, Man-cub!'

Mowgli looked – stared, rather – as insolently as he knew how, and in a minute Shere Khan turned away uneasily. 'Man-cub this, and Man-cub that,' he rumbled, going on with his drink, 'the cub is neither man nor cub, or he would have been afraid. Next season I shall have to beg his leave for a drink. *Augrh!*'

'That may come, too,' said Bagheera, looking him steadily between the eyes. 'That may come, too – Faugh, Shere Khan! – what new shame hast thou brought here?'

The Lame Tiger had dipped his chin and jowl in the water, and dark, oily streaks were floating from it downstream.

'Man!' said Shere Khan coolly. 'I killed an hour since.' He went on purring and growling to himself.

The line of beasts shook and wavered to and fro, and a whisper went up that grew to a cry: 'Man! Man! He has killed Man!' Then all looked towards Hathi, the Wild Elephant, but he seemed not to hear. Hathi never does anything till the time comes, and that is one of the reasons why he lives so long.

'At such a season as this to kill Man! Was no other game afoot?' said Bagheera scornfully, drawing himself out of the tainted water, and shaking each paw, cat-fashion, as he did so.

'I killed for choice – not for food.' The horrified whisper began again, and Hathi's watchful little white eye cocked itself in Shere Khan's direction. 'For choice,' Shere Khan drawled. 'Now come I to drink and make me clean again. Is there any to forbid?'

Bagheera's back began to curve like a bamboo in a high wind, but Hathi lifted up his trunk and spoke quietly.

'Thy kill was from choice?' he asked; and when Hathi asks a question it is best to answer.

'Even so. It was my right and my Night. Thou knowest, O Hathi.' Shere Khan spoke almost courteously.

'Yes, I know,' Hathi answered; and, after a little silence, 'Hast thou drunk thy fill?'

'For tonight, yes.'

'Go, then. The river is to drink, and not to defile. None but the Lame Tiger would so have boasted of his right at this season when – when we suffer together – Man and Jungle-People alike. Clean or unclean, get to thy lair, Shere Khan!'

The last words rang out like silver trumpets, and Hathi's three sons rolled forward half a pace, though there was no need. Shere Khan slunk away, not daring to growl, for he knew – what every one else knows – that when the last comes to the last, Hathi is the Master of the Jungle.

'What is this right Shere Khan speaks of?' Mowgli whispered in Bagheera's ear. 'To kill Man is *always* shameful. The Law says so. And yet Hathi says –'

'Ask him. I do not know, Little Brother. Right or no right, if Hathi had not spoken I would have taught that lame butcher his lesson. To come to the Peace Rock fresh from a kill of Man – and to boast of it – is a jackal's trick. Besides, he tainted the good water.'

Mowgli waited for a minute to pick up his courage, because no one cared to address Hathi directly, and then he cried: 'What is Shere Khan's right, O Hathi?' Both banks echoed his words, for all the People of the Jungle are intensely curious, and they had just seen something that none, except Baloo, who looked very thoughtful, seemed to understand.

'It is an old tale,' said Hathi; 'a tale older than the Jungle. Keep silence along the banks, and I will tell that tale.'

There was a minute or two of pushing and shouldering among the pig and the buffalo, and then the leaders of the herds grunted, one after another, 'We wait,' and Hathi strode forward till he was nearly knee-deep in the pool by the Peace Rock. Lean and wrinkled and yellow-tusked though he was, he looked what the Jungle knew him to be – their master.

'Ye know, children,' he began, 'that of all things ye most fear Man'; and there was a mutter of agreement.

'This tale touches thee, Little Brother,' said Bagheera to Mowgli.

'I? I am of the Pack – a hunter of the Free People,' Mowgli answered. 'What have I to do with Man?'

'And ye do not know why ye fear Man?' Hathi went on. 'This is the reason. In the beginning of the Jungle, and none know when that was, we of the Jungle walked together, having no fear of one another. In those days there was no drought, and leaves and flowers and fruit grew on the same tree, and we ate nothing at all except leaves and flowers and grass and fruit and bark.'

'I am glad I was not born in those days,' said Bagheera. 'Bark is only good to sharpen claws.'

'And the Lord of the Jungle was Tha, the First of the Elephants. He drew the Jungle out of deep waters with his trunk; and where he made furrows in the ground with his tusks, there the rivers ran; and where he struck with his foot, there rose ponds of good water; and when he blew through his trunk – thus – the trees fell. That was the manner in which the Jungle was made by Tha; and so the tale was told to me.'

'It has not lost fat in the telling,' Bagheera whispered, and Mowgli laughed behind his hand.

'In those days there was no corn or melons or pepper or sugar-cane, nor were there any little huts such as ye have all seen; and the Jungle-People knew nothing of Man, but lived in the Jungle together, making one people. But presently they began to dispute over their food, though there was grazing enough for all. They were lazy. Each wished to eat where he lay, as sometimes we can do now when the spring Rains are good. Tha, the First of the Elephants, was busy making new jungles and leading the rivers in their beds. He could not walk in all places; therefore he made the First of the Tigers the master and the judge of the Jungle, to whom the Jungle-People should bring their disputes. In those days the First of the Tigers ate fruit and grass with the others. He was as large as I am, and he was very beautiful, in colour all over like the blossom of the yellow creeper. There was never stripe nor bar upon his hide in those good days when this the Jungle was new. All the Jungle-People came before him without fear, and his word was the Law of all the Jungle. We were then, remember ye, one people.

'Yet upon a night there was a dispute between two bucks – a grazing-quarrel such as ye now settle with the horns and the fore-feet – and it is said that as the two spoke together before the First of the Tigers lying among the flowers, a buck pushed him with his horns, and the First of the Tigers forgot that he was the master and judge of the Jungle, and, leaping upon that buck, broke his neck.

'Till that night never one of us had died, and the First of the Tigers, seeing what he had done, and being made foolish by the scent of the blood, ran away into the Marshes of the North, and we of the Jungle, left without a judge, fell to fighting among ourselves; and Tha heard the noise of it and came back. Then some of us said this and some of us said that, but he saw the dead buck among the flowers, and asked who had killed, and we of the Jungle would not tell because the smell of the blood made us foolish. We ran to and fro in circles, capering and crying out and shaking our heads. Then Tha gave an order to the trees that hang low, and to the trailing creepers of the Jungle, that they should mark the killer of the buck so that he should know him again, and he said, "Who will now be master of the Jungle-People?" Then up leaped the Grey Ape who lives in the branches, and said, "I will now be master of the Jungle." At this Tha laughed, and said, "So be it," and went away very angry.

'Children, ye know the Grey Ape. He was then as he is now. At the first he made a wise face for himself, but in a little while he began to scratch and to leap up and down, and when Tha came back he found the Grey Ape hanging, head down, from a bough, mocking those who stood below; and they mocked him again. And so there was no Law in the Jungle – only foolish talk and senseless words.

'Then Tha called us all together and said: "The first of your masters has brought Death into the Jungle, and the second Shame. Now it is time there was a Law, and a Law that ye must not break. Now ye shall know Fear, and when ye have found him ye shall know that he is your master, and the rest shall follow." Then we of the Jungle said, "What is Fear?" And Tha said, "Seek till ye find." So we went up and down the Jungle seeking for Fear, and presently the buffaloes –'

'Ugh!' said Mysa, the leader of the buffaloes, from their sand-bank.

'Yes, Mysa, it was the buffaloes. They came back with the news that in a cave in the Jungle sat Fear, and that he had no hair, and went upon his hind legs. Then we of the Jungle followed the herd till we came to that cave, and Fear stood at the mouth of it, and he was, as the buffaloes had said, hairless, and he walked upon his hinder legs. When he saw us he cried out, and his voice filled us with the fear that we have now of that voice when we hear it, and we ran away, tramping upon and tearing each other because we were afraid. That night, so it was told to me, we of the

Jungle did not lie down together as used to be our custom, but each tribe drew off by itself – the pig with the pig, the deer with the deer; horn to horn, hoof to hoof – like keeping to like, and so lay shaking in the Jungle.

'Only the First of the Tigers was not with us, for he was still hidden in the Marshes of the North, and when word was brought to him of the Thing we had seen in the cave, he said: "I will go to this Thing and break his neck." So he ran all the night till he came to the cave; but the trees and the creepers on his path, remembering the order that Tha had given, let down their branches and marked him as he ran, drawing their fingers across his back, his flank, his forehead, and his jowl. Wherever they touched him there was a mark and a stripe upon his yellow hide. *And those stripes do his children wear to this day!* When he came to the cave, Fear, the Hairless One, put out his hand and called him "The Striped One that comes by night," and the First of the Tigers was afraid of the Hairless One, and ran back to the swamps howling.'

Mowgli chuckled quietly here, his chin in the water.

'So loud did he howl that Tha heard him and said, "What is the sorrow?" And the First of the Tigers, lifting up his muzzle to the new-made sky, which is now so old, said: "Give me back my power, O Tha. I am made ashamed before all the Jungle, and I have run away from a Hairless One, and he has called me a shameful name." "And why?" said Tha. "Because I am smeared with the mud of the marshes," said the First of the Tigers. "Swim, then, and roll on the wet grass, and if it be mud it will wash away," said Tha; and the First of the Tigers swam, and rolled and rolled upon the grass, till the Jungle ran round and round before his eyes, but not one little bar upon all his hide was changed, and Tha, watching him, laughed. Then the First of the Tigers said, "What have I done that this comes to me?" Tha said, "Thou hast killed the buck, and thou hast let Death loose in the Jungle, and with Death has come Fear, so that the People of the Jungle are afraid one of the other, as thou art afraid of the Hairless One." The First of the Tigers said, "They will never fear me, for I knew them since the beginning." Tha said, "Go and see." And the First of the Tigers ran to and fro, calling aloud to the deer and the pig and the sambhur and the porcupine and all the Jungle Peoples, and they all ran away from him who had been their judge, because they were afraid.

'Then the First of the Tigers came back, and his pride was broken in him, and, beating his head upon the ground, he tore up the earth with all his feet and said: "Remember that I was once the Master of the Jungle. Do not forget me, O Tha! Let my children remember that I was once without shame or fear!" And Tha said: "This much I will do, because thou and I together saw the Jungle made. For one night in each year it shall be as it was before the buck was killed – for thee and for thy children. In that one night, if ye meet the Hairless One – and his name is Man – ye shall not be afraid of him, but he shall be afraid of you, as though ye were judges of the Jungle and masters of all things. Show him mercy in that night of his fear, for thou hast known what Fear is."

'Then the First of the Tigers answered, "I am content"; but when next he drank he saw the black stripes upon his flank and his side, and he remembered the name that the Hairless One had given him, and he was angry. For a year he lived in the marshes, waiting till Tha should keep his promise. And upon a night when the Jackal of the Moon [the Evening Star] stood clear of the Jungle, he felt that his Night was upon him, and he went to that cave to meet the Hairless One. Then it happened as Tha promised, for the Hairless One fell down before him and lay along the ground, and the First of the Tigers struck him and broke his back, for he thought that there was but one such Thing in the Jungle, and that he had killed Fear. Then, nosing above the kill, he heard Tha coming down from the woods of the North, and presently the voice of the First of the Elephants, which is the voice that we hear now –'

The thunder was rolling up and down the dry, scarred hills, but it brought no rain – only heat-lightning that flickered along the ridges – and Hathi went on: '*That* was the voice he heard, and it said: "Is this thy mercy?" The First of the Tigers licked his lips and said: "What matter? I have killed Fear." And Tha said: "O blind and foolish! Thou hast untied the feet of Death, and he will follow thy trail till thou diest. Thou hast taught Man to kill!"'

'The First of the Tigers, standing stiffly to his kill, said: "He is as the buck was. There is no Fear. Now I will judge the Jungle Peoples once more."'

'And Tha said: "Never again shall the Jungle Peoples come to thee. They shall never cross thy trail, nor sleep near thee, nor follow after thee, nor browse by thy lair. Only Fear shall follow thee, and with a blow that thou canst not see he shall bid thee wait his pleasure. He shall make the ground to open under thy feet, and the creepers to twist about thy neck, and the tree-trunks to grow together about thee higher than thou canst leap, and at the last he shall take thy hide to wrap his cubs when they are cold. Thou hast shown him no mercy, and none will he show thee.'

'The First of the Tigers was very bold, for his Night was still on him, and he said: "The Promise of Tha is the Promise of Tha. He will not take away my Night?" And Tha said: "The one Night is thine, as I have said, but there is a price to pay. Thou hast taught Man to kill, and he is no slow learner."'

'The First of the Tigers said: "He is here under my foot, and his back is broken. Let the Jungle know I have killed Fear."'

'Then Tha laughed, and said: "Thou hast killed one of many, but thou thyself shalt tell the Jungle – for thy Night is ended."'

'So the day came; and from the mouth of the cave went out another Hairless One, and he saw the kill in the path, and the First of the Tigers above it, and he took a pointed stick –'

'They throw a thing that cuts now,' said Ikki, rustling down the bank; for Ikki was considered uncommonly good eating by the Gonds – they called him Ho-Igoo – and he knew something of the wicked little Gondee axe that whirls across a clearing like a dragon-fly.

'It was a pointed stick, such as they put in the foot of a pittrap,' said Hathi, 'and throwing it, he struck the First of the Tigers deep in the flank. Thus it happened as Tha said, for the First of the Tigers ran howling up and down the Jungle till he tore out the stick, and all the Jungle knew that the Hairless One could strike from far off, and they feared more than before. So it came about that the First of the Tigers taught the Hairless One to kill – and ye know what harm that has since done to all our peoples – through the noose, and the pitfall, and the hidden trap, and the flying stick, and the stinging fly that comes out of white smoke [Hathi meant the rifle], and the Red Flower that drives us into the open. Yet for one night in the year the Hairless One fears the Tiger, as Tha promised, and never has the Tiger given him cause to be less afraid. Where he finds him, there he kills him, remembering how the First of the Tigers was made ashamed. For the rest, Fear walks up and down the Jungle by day and by night.'

'Ahi! Aoo!' said the deer, thinking of what it all meant to them.

'And only when there is one great Fear over all, as there is now, can we of the Jungle lay aside our little fears, and meet together in one place as we do now.'

'For one night only does Man fear the Tiger?' said Mowgli.

'For one night only,' said Hathi.

'But I – but we – but all the Jungle knows that Shere Khan kills Man twice and thrice in a moon.'

'Even so. Then he springs from behind and turns his head aside as he strikes, for he is full of fear. If Man looked at him he would run. But on his one Night he goes openly down to the village. He walks between the houses and thrusts his head into the doorway, and the men fall on their faces, and there he does his kill. One kill in that Night.'

'Oh!' said Mowgli to himself, rolling over in the water. 'Now I see why it was Shere Khan bade me look at him! He got no good of it, for he could not hold his eyes steady, and – and I certainly did not fall down at his feet. But then I am not a man, being of the Free people.'

'Umm!' said Bagheera deep in his furry throat. 'Does the Tiger know his Night?'

'Never till the Jackal of the Moon stands clear of the evening mist. Sometimes it falls in the dry summer and sometimes in the wet rains – this one Night of the Tiger. But for the First of the Tigers, this would never have been, nor would any of us have known fear.'

The deer grunted sorrowfully, and Bagheera's lips curled in a wicked smile. 'Do men know this – tale?' said he.

'None know it except the tigers, and we, the elephants – the children of Tha. Now ye by the pools have heard it, and I have spoken.'

Hathi dipped his trunk into the water as a sign that he did not wish to talk.

'But – but – but,' said Mowgli, turning to Baloo, 'why did not the First of the Tigers continue to eat grass and leaves and trees? He did but break the buck's neck. He did not *eat*. What led him to the hot meat?'

'The trees and the creepers marked him, Little Brother, and made him the striped thing that we see. Never again would he eat their fruit; but from that day he revenged himself upon the deer, and the others, the Eaters of Grass,' said Baloo.

'Then *thou* knowest the tale. Heh? Why have I never heard?'

'Because the Jungle is full of such tales. If I made a beginning there would never be an end to them. Let go my ear, Little Brother.'

THE LAW OF THE JUNGLE

Just to give you an idea of the immense variety of the Jungle Law, I have translated into verse (Baloo always recited them in a sort of sing-song) a few of the laws that apply to the wolves. There are, of course, hundreds and hundreds more, but these will do for specimens of the simpler rulings.

Now this is the Law of the Jungle – as old and as true as the sky;
And the Wolf that shall keep it may prosper, but the Wolf that shall break it must die.

As the creeper that girdles the tree-trunk, the Law runneth forward and back –
For the strength of the Pack is the Wolf, and the strength of the Wolf is the Pack.

Wash daily from nose-tip to tail-tip; drink deeply, but never too deep;
And remember the night is for hunting, and forget not the day is for sleep.

The Jackal may follow the Tiger, but, Cub, when thy whiskers are grown,
Remember the Wolf is a hunter – go forth and get food of thine own.

Keep peace with the Lords of the Jungle – the Tiger, the Panther, the Bear;
And trouble not Hathi the Silent, and mock not the Boar in his lair.

When Pack meets with Pack in the Jungle, and neither will go from the trail,
Lie down till the leaders have spoken – it may be fair words shall prevail.

When ye fight with a Wolf of the Pack, ye must fight him alone and afar,
Lest others take part in the quarrel, and the Pack be diminished by war.

The Lair of the Wolf is his refuge, and where he has made him his home,

Not even the Head Wolf may enter, not even the Council
    may come.

The Lair of the Wolf is his refuge, but where he has digged
    it too plain,
The Council shall send him a message, and so he shall
    change it again.

If ye kill before midnight, be silent, and wake not the
    woods with your bay,
Lest ye frighten the deer from the crops, and the brothers
    go empty away.

JAN MARK

Hide-and-Seek

Schoolboy Mark hatches a clever plot to protect
vulnerable wildlife from destruction at the
hands of a mindless bully . . . even if it means
putting his friends at risk . . .

Jan Mark has written this story specially for
the anthology.

A GORILLA   A HOLDSTOCK

PPARENTLY VANDALS come in three varieties.
The Grade One vandal is the kind who demolishes a
telephone box for the same reason that people
climb Mount Everest; because it is there, due to some inner
urge, perhaps. Grade Two vandals wreck things because
they happen to be passing and, anyway, there is nothing
better to do. Then there are the Big Business Grade Three
vandals who cannot see the word 'park' without thinking
how much better it would look with 'car' written in front
of it.

It was the Grade Three vandals who eventually finished
off Rough Lots, but we didn't come across many of that type
at school. I'd never have thought of classifying vandals
anyway, until Mark Murray did his wildlife project in the
Fourth Year. The whole class had to produce a project
during the Easter term and most of us chose frogs, but Mark
did vandals. Mr Blunt, who was our teacher that year, had a
sense of humour and Mark might have got away with it,
only he named names. Among other things, he devoted a

whole page to the Great Crested Vandal and used Adam Holdstock, from 4j, as an example, with illustrations. Adam was easy to draw, even if you were no good at drawing, and Mark was; partly because he looked rather like a cartoon character anyway, having very small eyes that might have been put in with a paper punch, and partly because of the crest which was black and spiky. He wore army boots – even in 4j he was already big enough – and he couldn't see a caterpillar without jumping on it.

Mark's vandal project was beautifully done, the best in the class, and if he had stuck to frogs like the rest of us, it would have been put up on a display board in the entrance hall for Parents' Evening. Instead he got a long talk about libel from Mr Blunt.

'Suppose I put that up on the wall and Mrs Holdstock saw it?' Mr Blunt said.

'She ought to see it. Everybody ought to see it. The public should be told,' said Mark, who read a lot of newspapers. He remarked to me later that if Mrs Holdstock didn't know about Adam already she must be in a coma.

'The public doesn't *need* telling,' Mr Blunt said, 'and if the public gets to hear of your project we shall be all over the front page of the *Kent Messenger*.' So the vandal project was circulated privately round the class and Mark had it safely at home before Holdstock heard about it, which he did, in the end. Someone grassed.

'You been calling me a vandal?' demanded Holdstock, in his combat boots, when he waylaid me and Mark on the way home from school at the end of the Easter term.

'Who says so?' Mark said, getting ready for a sprint start.

'Everybody,' Holdstock said, gripping his spear. It was a green iron rail that he had nicked from the fence round the churchyard, quite blunt but very heavy, good for whopping things with. 'Everybody can't be wrong.'

'Why should I call you a vandal?' Mark asked, innocently smiling.

There was no answer to that, as Mark knew perfectly well, except, 'Because I am one', and while Holdstock was working that out we nipped round him and ran.

'You see,' Mark said, when we reached his house, '*he* doesn't think he's a vandal. He thinks he's a higher primate.'

'Like a gorilla?'

'*Not* like a gorilla,' Mark said. 'Gorillas are nice people. If you had to draw a chart' – Mark was very keen on charts – 'showing intelligent life forms, who would you put on top; a gorilla or Adam Holdstock?'

I had to agree; there was no contest and, anyway, I could see what Mark was getting at. The one thing that Holdstock could remember from RE lessons was the bit in the Bible where it says that God gave Adam dominion over every creeping thing that creepeth upon the earth.

'He didn't mean *you*,' the teacher said, when Holdstock celebrated that particular information by squashing a spider, but the damage was done.

'Adam was created *last*,' Mark said, when Adam reminded us of his dominion over creeping things. 'Last in, first out,' he added, darkly.

Mark intended to become a naturalist. When the rest of us were asked to write about what we wanted to be when we grew up, we said nurses or soccer stars or pop singers because the words were short and easy to spell. Susie Beale wanted to be a beautician and asked me how to write it, but I thought she said 'politician' and I couldn't spell that either. 'Just put MP,' I said, so Susie wrote: *I want to be an MP when I grow up so that I can make Ladies look pretty and do their hair nice and help them to not have blackheads.*

Mark wrote: *I want to be a naturalist*, in his best italic script, and the teacher was properly impressed, whereas she just thought Susie was wrong in the head. Mark spent a lot of time bird-watching and pond-dipping, and recorded his observations in tidy notebooks. He could easily have faked a frog project from those notebooks – he knew far more

about frogs than the rest of us – but instead he did vandals
and after that Adam Holdstock was on to him.

I didn't see much of Holdstock during the Easter holidays, but there were traces of him everywhere; splintered
saplings, trampled daffodils, ripped posters, broken glass.
When Mrs Elliot had the door of the Post Office painted
there were things found next morning, stuck to the wet
paint, and when my dad put down hard standing for the car,
personal remarks were written in the wet concrete. There
were also boot prints – which are still there. Holdstock's
boots featured prominently in Mark's project, as the spoor
of the Great Crested Vandal.

Most of the time, though, he was tracking Mark. I seldom
saw much of him, either. Although we lived quite close to
each other, we didn't meet very often except going to and
from school. I played a lot in the rec; Mark was never very
far away, but he had a different habitat. These days the
village is built up, part of the town, really, but at that time it
was just a triangle of streets with plenty of green spaces,
and between the rec and our school, where the hypermar-
ket and its car-park now stand, was a bit of land that seemed
to belong to no one. It was called Rough Lots. This was
Mark's habitat, and it was there that Holdstock followed
him.

Rough Lots had always been rough, but it had got a lot
rougher during the war, when the Home Guard dug ditches
all over it to practise trench warfare. Once it had been
thickly wooded, but the only trees still standing were
alders. The oaks and beeches had died or been cut down; all
that was left of them was toppling trunks, strung with ivy
and wild hops, or stumps that sprouted lush fat fungi after a
hot summer. Holdstock went there occasionally to perse-
cute frogs in the pond or smash the bracket fungi (*The
Great Crested Vandal is afraid of plants: that is why it kills
them*. Mark observed in his project), but it was a long walk,
by his standards, from the Holdstock house, and plenty of
vulnerable plants grew closer to home. But after Mark
published his project, Holdstock, boiling with vengeance,

followed him there, and all round the village. This was a
real hazard, especially as it was spring. Mark's nests were at
risk.

The path to school skirted the upper edge of Rough Lots,
but Holdstock was usually late for school and had to make
those last few hundred yards of the journey at a lumbering
trot. At home time a teacher patrolled the path to make
sure that we really did go home. People who had serious
business there, like Mark or the Chivers Gang, had to sneak
back afterwards. I think the reason that Holdstock never
bothered much with Rough Lots was that no one cared
what he did there. When he committed vandalous acts in
people's front gardens or in the street, he added to his awful
reputation. No one cared about Rough Lots, except Mark.

He had made a map of the place with every trench and
tree trunk noted and named. Some of the names were the
kind that you might find on an Ordnance Survey map:
Swamp Crossing, Devil's Ditch, Gorse Hill; others were
more particular. There was a beech trunk, grey and lean,
called Blunt Point, after our Mr Blunt, and a squat, knotted
oak stump that Mark had named the Holdstock Bulge. The
pond was Lake Murray. If you were a friend of Mark's or he
caught you doing something that he approved of, like
helping a toad across the street or rescuing a bird from a cat,
you might be rewarded by having a geographical feature
named after you. Susie Beale, MP, who could not spell but
was kind to crane-flies, had been immortalized at Cape
Beale, a little promontory on the shores of Lake Murray,
and the day I first saw Mark's map I noticed a bank named
Latham's Ridge. I asked him what I'd done to deserve
it.

'You don't like Holdstock,' Mark said, simply. I felt as if
I'd been given the Queen's Award for Industry without
even trying.

Mark rarely brought his notebooks to school, and never
the map, so early in the beginning of the summer term I
was surprised to see one of the books lying on his table in
class, and less surprised, half an hour later, to see Adam

Holdstock kicking it down the corridor. I grabbed Susie Beale and we rushed to the rescue, which was a stupid thing to do because the slightest opposition goaded Holdstock to madness. No one ever got close enough to Holdstock to see if his eyes were bloodshot – it wasn't necessary. He became bloodshot all over and went into overdrive. When we tried to stop him playing football with Mark's notebook, he put it into his mouth and began tugging at the pages with his teeth.

Mr Blunt came along at that moment. He sighed.

'Is that your own book you're trying to eat, Holdstock?' he said.

'It's Mark Murray's!' Susie yelled. I had told her about Cape Beale and she wanted to be worthy of the honour. 'He's trying to *destroy* it.'

'I can see that,' said Mr Blunt. He took hold of the book in one hand and Holdstock's collar in the other and shook them gently, the way you try to get a shoe away from a terrier. Holdstock was sent to stand outside the Headteacher's door, where he spent quite a lot of his time, and Mr Blunt handed the notebook to me and Susie for safekeeping.

It was a new one. Only a couple of pages had been written on in Mark's beautiful handwriting that was as clear as printing, but they were crumpled and soiled and bore the unmistakable spoor of the Great Crested Vandal. Mark supervised the school pond at break, so Susie and I took the notebook back to the classroom, with Mr Blunt's permission, and tried to tidy it up. We couldn't help reading it at the same time.

May 10:   Yellow-hammer in churchyard. Willow warbler in Mrs Capon's laburnum. RARE passenger pigeon in – (location secret). First sighting EVER in Kent. Must NOT reveal whereabouts.

May 13:   Now certain about passenger pigeon. This is an historic event in the history of ornithology. VITAL no one knows about it yet, especially A.H.

May 14:   TWO passenger pigeons seen near Blunt

Point. This is TREMENDOUS. Am certain they will mate. A.H. MUST NOT KNOW!!!!!

May 17: Saw BOTH passenger pigeons again this evening. Perhaps they were searching for nesting materials. Must build a hide and observe them.

Facts known about the passenger pigeon:
THOUGHT TO BE EXTINCT!!!!!!
Length: 42 cm including tail. Plumage: Grey. Blackish on tail. Breast lighter with pink tinge. Sheen on neck.
Habitat: Woods, gardens, scrubland (like Rough Lots).
VERY RARE IN KENT.
Nest: Twigs, grass and ferns. In trees. Eggs: White with black speckles. Late May.

Susie and I looked at each other.

'I'm sure passenger pigeons are extinct,' Susie said.

'Maybe he saw a wood pigeon and got excited,' I suggested, although it was unlike Mark to make this kind of mistake, but we were both worried, even if he did turn out to be wrong. We knew who A. H. was, and we knew that A.H. had seen these top-secret notes with their details of Mark's important discovery, and all those unfortunate remarks about how vital it was that A.H. should *not* see them. Whatever Mark had seen, it was clear that he had seen something, and we knew what would happen now because it had been happening all through the holidays. Holdstock would be looking for that nest and it could not be long before he found it. Mark hadn't quite told him where to look but it would not take even Holdstock long to work out that if he kept an eye on Mark, sooner or later Mark would lead him to the nest. When Mark came in from pond duty we were waiting for him in the corridor. Susie handed him the book.

'You left it lying around.'

Mark seized it and made loud noises of relief. Further along the corridor was Holdstock, waiting outside the Head's room. He was watching us. Mark wiped imaginary sweat beads from his forehead.

'Holdstock had it. I think he's read it,' I said.

'About the passenger pigeons?'

'Yes. And I bet he works out where to find them. He'll follow you. Fancy bringing it to school.'

'I thought the passenger pigeon was extinct,' Susie said.

'I didn't want to let it out of my sight,' Mark said. In that case, I thought that he had been criminally careless, but I didn't say so. Knowing that Holdstock had had his hands – and boots – on it was punishment enough.

'I'll have to take you into my confidence,' Mark said. Susie and I had thought we *were* in his confidence, not just on his map, but we had to look flattered. 'We must mount a twenty-four hour guard on that nest.'

'Twenty-four hours?' Susie said. '*All night?*'

'Not exactly,' said Mark. We were round the corner now, out of Holdstock's view. 'Even the Great Crested Vandal retires to its den at night. And he can't do anything during school time; but every other minute we must keep watch.'

He squared his jaw. This was serious stuff; a plan of campaign.

'On Holdstock?'

'And the nest.'

'You mean, you'll show it to us?' I said.

'It *can't* be a passenger pigeon,' Susie said. 'I'm sure they're extinct.'

'I'll show you where it is,' Mark said, taking no notice of Susie. He, after all, was the naturalist. What did an aspiring beautician know about pigeons?

'Have you built the hide?'

'Did you read *all* of it?' Mark said, in a betrayed voice.

'Not properly,' Susie said, quickly, in case he changed his mind about trusting us. 'But we couldn't help seeing bits – where we were flattening out the creases.'

'You'll have to swear not to reveal its whereabouts.'

We swore. We swore to keep silent or hurl ourselves into the Pit of Vandals, which was a corner of Rough Lots given over to fly tipping. It was a serious oath. We went to the Pit of Vandals only to stare in horrid fascination and give ourselves nightmares. The passenger pigeons were safe with us.

We made an effort to be especially good that afternoon so that we would be let out first. There was no chance at all that Holdstock would be let out first from *his* class, but Mark wanted a head start on the rest of the school, so that we could be safely in Rough Lots before the teacher on duty got far enough along the footpath to see what we were up to. A chestnut paling fence lounged down the side of the path, and although Holdstock and lesser vandals regularly armed themselves with staves pulled out of it, there was only one place where you could get through easily and fortunately it was beyond a slight bend and masked by a wild buddleia bush. By the time the duty teacher, who was Mrs Caldwell today (namesake of Caldwell's Dyke, a murky ditch near Lake Murray), had strolled as far as the buddleia, we were through the gap and out of sight among the bushes and ferns.

There were many little paths worn between the bushes. I expected Mark to avoid a well-trodden way, but he followed a wide track that ran downhill in the direction of Latham's Ridge. I knew from the map that this was the M 1. Mark had named all the tracks 'M' something – M for Murray, naturally – and the M 1 was the widest.

'Shouldn't we stick to the side paths?' Susie said. 'Someone might see us. Holdstock's lot might.'

Holdstock had henchmen. They were Grade Two vandals in Mark's scheme of things, but where Holdstock led they were seldom far behind. Even now they might have been detailed to watch us. I looked over my shoulder to see if anyone was following, but at that moment Mark turned and plunged in among the bracken. Susie followed. This was not one of the M class tracks; it was barely a B road and looked newly made. Bent double, we were creeping through a tunnel under the bracken fronds, in the bitter-smelling half-light between the stems. We came out on the south shore of Lake Murray where there was a clearing and, beyond it, on the far side of the lake and on the very boundary of Rough Lots, a row of alder trees. Close by, among the bracken, stood what looked like a compost heap topped with a shaggy thatch of ferns.

'Is that the hide?' Susie said. 'I thought you weren't meant to be able to see hides.'

'It's the birds that aren't meant to be able to see them,' Mark said.

'But you don't want *people* to see this one,' I said. 'Anyway, if you just hid in the bracken the birds wouldn't see you.'

'Birds have very sharp eyes,' Mark said.

'Then they'll be able to see us now,' Susie said.

'That doesn't matter at the moment,' said Mark, 'but if they saw us every day they'd get suspicious. They might abandon the nest.'

'Where is this nest, then?'

'There isn't much to see yet, they're still building it,' Mark said, as if apologizing for his friends. 'Come into the hide and I'll show you.'

The hide was scarcely big enough for one, let alone three, but as Mark pointed out, usually there would be only one of us in it anyway. It was the sort of hut everyone builds on rough ground – the Chivers Gang had a kind of shanty town – but it was rather like an army pillbox in construction, with a concealed entrance and a horizontal slit to look out of.

'See those two alders,' Mark said, pointing in the direction of the boundary fence. 'Look at the right-hand tree, where the trunk forks . . . see that grass? That's the beginning of the nest.'

We looked. Only a budding naturalist like Mark would have guessed that the wisps of dried grass, twigs and fern fronds were a nest, but then, as it said in the notebook, *he* had seen the passenger pigeons starting to build it. Of the pigeons themselves there was no sign.

'They're mainly active early in the morning and at late evening,' Mark said, in textbook tones. 'I was lucky to see them at all. But look, it doesn't matter so much about watching *them*. What we've got to do is make sure no one else finds them.'

'But Holdstock knows about them now,' I said.

'He wouldn't, if you hadn't written it all down,' Susie said.

'He's the one we've got to look out for,' Mark said, scowling at Susie. 'We'll call it Operation Holdstock-Watch. There must be someone posted in Rough Lots at all times.'

I could imagine us building another hide to watch the first hide from, and then a third hide, in order to watch the second, until we ended up with a housing estate, like the Chivers Gang. In the end we worked out a rota. Mark undertook the first watch until 8 a.m., which was easy for him as his mother was used to his getting up early to observe the dawn habits of slugs and so forth; and the late shift for much the same reason. In autumn he was often seen lurking in the street long after the rest of us had been called in, hunting for bats. Susie and I were to share the 8–9 shift and also to take turns from 4.30 till 7.30, relieving each other in time for tea. All three of us would be there for the most dangerous shift of all, 3.30 till 4.30, when the Great Crested Vandal was most in evidence.

The plan worked well for the next five days because Holdstock was much slower at working out where we were than we had given him credit for. He popped up all over the place, behind hedges and telephone boxes – which enjoyed a close season while he was otherwise engaged – in ditches, up trees. There were now three of us to follow and he always seemed to pick the one who was going home, or fetching the shopping, but finally, on Friday evening, he ran us to earth. It was 5.30. Mark had already left for his tea and I was waiting to be relieved by Susie, getting very impatient. The weather was warm and Lake Murray didn't smell any too wholesome. Just after she arrived we heard rustling in the bracken.

'You were followed,' I said.

'Holdstock!' Susie said and dived into the hide, but it was Mark himself who came out of the tunnel. He hurled himself into the hide with us. It was like three tortoises sharing the same shell. It bulged.

'Holdstock's here.'

'Where?'

'Up by Mount Murray. I came to warn you.'

'What are you doing here anyway?' Susie demanded. 'You're not due on for ages, yet.'

'I was passing,' Mark said, vaguely. We didn't ask what he had been passing because the footpath led only to the school. I guessed that he had been unable to keep away and that, loitering wistfully, he had unwittingly led Holdstock to the spot.

'We'll have to be extra vigilant now,' he said, as if it were our fault.

'I've got to go and have tea soon,' I said. 'My mum'll go spare if I'm late. She'll think I've gone off with someone.'

'We'll create a diversion,' Mark said. 'Wait a few minutes for me and Susie to head him off and then you can run for it. You can lure him away.'

He shot off into the tunnel with Susie. I was left in the hide with my back to the observation slit, keeping a weather eye on the tunnel in case Holdstock came out of it. In any case, there was nothing much to see through the slit. In the mornings, when I relieved Mark, I noticed that the nest had got bigger. It was beginning to look like a nest and it was much more obvious, but Susie and I were not allowed to go up close for a proper examination in case we frightened the passenger pigeons. We had neither of us seen the pigeons at all, but they were clearly somewhere about, because of the nest growing bigger.

Have you ever been in the London Underground just before a train comes into the station? There's a mighty rushing wind. I *felt* Holdstock coming before he appeared, so I was ready when he shot out of the tunnel, just like a tube train. He skidded to a halt, looked round and yelled, 'I can see you!'

I knew he didn't mean me because he was facing the other way. In fact, he wasn't talking to anyone in particular. 'I'll get you! I'll get your stupid pigeons! Yaaaaar! Look out, pigeons! Yaaaaar! Stupid Murray!' Like a charging rhinoceros that cannot be diverted, he cantered across the clearing and disappeared among the bushes. I could hear him crashing about in the undergrowth. Small clods of earth dropped from Cape Beale into the still waters of Lake Murray and ripples spread. As the sounds of his onslaught died away, Mark came out of the tunnel.

'That was Holdstock,' I said.

'He'll be back,' said Mark. He sounded almost hopeful and I suspected that he was really enjoying this undercover guerrilla warfare. As a naturalist he seldom saw active service and the Chiverses wouldn't have him in their gang. They thought he was a nutter. So did I, sometimes.

The weekend rota meant heavy duty for all of us. When I went to take over from Susie at 10 o'clock next morning, I noticed the spoor of the Great Crested Vandal in the mud round the gap in the fence. Broken branches and bruised ferns along the M1 were further proof of his presence, but clearly he hadn't been back to Lake Murray, for as I came out of the tunnel I saw that the hide was still standing. Susie, very excited, beckoned me in and pointed through the slit. 'They've laid!'

'They've what?'

'They've laid an egg.'

I looked at the alder fork. Since I was last there the nest had become a positive hayrick with half-timbering, and perched on top, in a small dent, lay a single egg. It was a surprisingly large egg for a bird reputed to be only 42 centimetres long including tail; even from that distance it looked to me about the size of a hen's egg, but white. I could just make out faint black spots.

'Have they abandoned the nest?' I said.

'Why should they?'

'Well, birds usually sit on eggs once they've laid them.'

'Perhaps they haven't finished. Perhaps they don't start

sitting till they've laid them all,' Susie suggested. 'It's nice and sunny. It won't get cold.'

She went away and I settled down to wait. I sat with my eyes to the slit for fifty-five minutes and never once saw the male or female passenger pigeon, but from time to time I heard the Great Crested Vandal in the bushes and once he came as close as the farther shore of Lake Murray, where he paused to chuck in a Coke can; but he didn't see the hide.

It was the next day that he found it. We were all there; Mark had just arrived and we were changing shifts when Holdstock prowled into the clearing. When he saw the three of us together he came walloping over to investigate.

'That your den?' he said, stepping back a pace to get a good run at it.

I was about to say yes and let him get on with the demolition so that he would go away, when Mark said, 'No, it's a hide.'

Holdstock paused, one boot raised as if he were about to paw the ground and snort steam from his nostrils. 'What you watch birds from?' he said.

'That's right,' Mark said, and bravely stepped in front of it. Holdstock shouldered him aside and scrambled into the hide. It rocked and shuddered. Holdstock's arm appeared through the slit, pointing.

'That the nest?'

'What nest?' Susie said, innocently, but Holdstock was not fooled.

'That thingy pigeon Murray's been hiding.' He rose upright. The hide disintegrated round him and he stood there with twigs and fern fronds hanging from his head and shoulders, a terrifying sight, like a heathen idol that someone had conjured to life. Then he ran, through the bracken, across Caldwell's Dyke, straight for the alder trees where the nest of the passenger pigeons lay unprotected among the leaves, and all those days of patient work at early morning and late evening, gathering twigs and ferns and grass, were laid waste in a second with one blow from Holdstock's horrible fist.

Then he came back to us, quite calmly, walking. As he went past he gave Mark a shove.

'Who's a vandal, then?' he said; and went.

We stood there. Susie began to cry. Mark bowed his head and walked over to the remains of the nest along the track that Holdstock had smashed through the bracken. I followed him. The nest, reduced to hay and sticks, lay all round the foot of the alder. In the middle of the wreck lay a fragment of white shell with black freckles.

Susie came up behind us, still crying. I thought Mark might cry too, but he looked resigned, cheerful even. 'Some you win, some you lose,' said Mark. 'Come on, I've got something to show you.'

Thinking that perhaps grief had numbed him, we followed Mark forlornly through the bracken tunnel for the last time, up the M1 and on to the footpath. Mark turned right, towards the road. There was a house on the corner with a long garden that ran the width of the rec. Part of it was concealed behind a high wooden fence, but near the house there was only a low stone wall with a cotoneaster growing across it. Mark reached over the wall and lifted a branch of the cotoneaster. Under it, built on to the branch below, was an empty nest.

'Did he get that too?' Susie said.

'No,' said Mark. 'He never knew it was there. He's been too busy hunting for passenger pigeons. This lot flew this morning. I was coming to tell you.'

'What were they?' I said.

'Blackbirds,' said Mark. 'She must have built her nest in the Easter holidays I expect, when there was no one about. She must have had a shock when we all started going to school again. I was dead scared Holdstock would find it.'

'He found the passenger pigeons instead,' Susie said. She couldn't help adding, 'I don't believe they *were* passenger pigeons, but he got them, anyway.'

'He thinks he did,' Mark said. He grinned. 'It's called drawing fire.' Susie thought he meant drawing with a pencil and screwed her finger into her forehead. I looked at the grin. I looked at the empty nest.

'There weren't any passenger pigeons, were there?'

'There were once,' Mark said.

'*Told* you they were extinct,' Susie said, then she glared at him. 'You didn't see anything, did you?'

'Yes, well; not –'

'*You* built the nest.'

'Yes, but it –'

'Every day, when we weren't there.'

'He laid the egg as well,' I said, bitterly. I felt we had been used, exposed unnecessarily to peril, possible death, even, at the boots of Holdstock.

'I got it out of the fridge and . . . made improvements.'

'I suppose that notebook was a plant, too. Holdstock was meant to see it?' Susie, like me, was remembering all the heart-stopping moments while we cowered in the hide when Holdstock was on the rampage. 'All that, for a bunch of blackbirds?'

'Just till they were fledged,' Mark said. 'He can't get them now.'

'But, blackbirds! There's millions of blackbirds.'

'There were millions of passenger pigeons once,' Mark said. 'Now they're extinct – but there's millions of Holdstocks.'

It was the voice of a naturalist speaking, but when Mark finally did leave school he went into the army and was last heard of yomping across East Falkland, where there are no passenger pigeons either, but plenty of penguins. His mother says he likes being a soldier. I'm not surprised, to tell you the truth. In a way, you could see it coming. Perhaps he really meant to write 'strategist' that time, only he couldn't spell it.

GERALD DURRELL

The Bay of Olives

from *Birds, Beasts and Relatives*

Most of us have seen wonders of the natural world on television – wide-angled, sweeping shots of shimmering prairies; glorious technicolour close-ups of intricate insects pinpointed by a zoom lens.

But if you give yourself a bit of time outside, on your own, tucked away from noisy distractions, you'll find that you are already equipped with all the highly sensitive instruments (eyes, ears, nose, mouth, skin and brain) needed to enjoy the hidden entertainment that lies all around. Empty field or overgrown garden; old wasteland or leafy park: the three-dimensional, multi-sensual, unedited experience of the natural world in action is on at a quiet spot near you, twenty-four hours a day!

Gerald Durrell made just this discovery when he was a boy, with a bit of help from an imaginative teacher called George. In this true and funny anecdote, Gerald and Roger (his dog) go exploring on the Greek island of Corfu . . .

AS YOU LEFT THE VILLA and walked down through the olive groves, you eventually reached the road with its thick coating of white dust, soft as silk. If you walked along this for half a mile or so, you came to a goat track which led down a steep slope through the olives and then you reached a small half-moon bay, rimmed with white sands and great piles of dried ribbon weed that had been thrown up by the winter storms and lay along the beach like large, badly made birds' nests. The two arms of the bay were composed of small cliffs, at the base of which were innumerable rock pools, filled with the glint and glitter of sea life.

As soon as George realized that to incarcerate me every morning of the week in the villa impaired my concentration, he instituted the novel educational gambit of 'outdoor lessons'. The sandy beach and the shaggy piles of weed soon became scorching deserts or impenetrable jungles and, with the aid of a reluctant crab or sand-hopper to play the part of Cortez or Marco Polo, we would explore them diligently. Geography lessons done under these circumstances I found had immense charm. We once decided, with the aid of rocks, to do a map of the world along the edge of the sea, so that we had real sea. It was an immensely absorbing task for, to begin with, it was not all that easy to find rocks shaped like Africa or India or South America, and sometimes two or three rocks had to be joined together to give the required shape to the continent. Then, of course, when you were obtaining a rock, you turned it over very carefully and found a host of sea life underneath it which would keep us both happily absorbed for a quarter of an hour or so, till George realized with a start that this was not getting on with our map of the world.

This little bay became one of my favourite haunts and nearly every afternoon while the family were having their siesta, Roger and I would make our way down through the breathless olive groves, vibrating with the cries of the cicadas, and pad our way along the dusty road, Roger sneezing voluptuously as his great paws stirred up the dust which went up his nose like snuff. Once we reached the bay, whose waters in the afternoon sun were so still and transparent they did not seem to be there at all, we would swim for a while in the shallows and then each of us would go about his own particular hobbies.

For Roger, this consisted of desperate and unsuccessful attempts to catch some of the small fish that flicked and trembled in the shallow water. He would stalk along slowly, muttering to himself, his ears cocked, gazing down into the water. Then, suddenly, he would plunge his head beneath the surface and you heard his jaws clop together and he would pull his head out, sneeze violently and shake the water off his fur, while the goby or blenny that he had attempted to catch would flip a couple of yards farther on and squat on a rock pouting at him and trembling its tail seductively.

For me the tiny bay was so full of life that I scarcely knew where to begin my collecting. Under and on top of the rocks were the chalky white tunnels of the tube worms, like some swirling and complicated pattern of icing sugar on a cake, and in the slightly deeper water there were stuck in the sand what appeared to be lengths of miniature hose pipe. If you stood and watched carefully, a delicate, feathery, flower-like cluster of tentacles would appear at the ends of the hose pipes – tentacles of iridescent blue and red and brown that would turn slowly round and round. These were the bristle worms; a rather ugly name, I felt, for such a beautiful creature. Sometimes there would be little clusters of them and they looked like a flower bed whose flowers could move. You had to approach them with infinite caution, for should you move your feet too rapidly through the water you would set up currents that telegraphed your approach and the tentacles would bunch together and dive with incredible speed back into the tube.

Here and there on the sandy floor of the bay were half-moons of black, shiny ribbon weed looking like dark feather boas, anchored to the sand, and in these you would find pipe fish, whose heads looked extraordinarily like elongated sea horses, perched on the end of a long, slender body. The pipe fishes would float upright among the ribbon weed which they resembled so closely that it required a lot of concentrated searching to find them.

Along the shore, under the rocks, you could find tiny crabs or beadlet anemones like little scarlet and blue jewelled pincushions, or the snakelocks anemones, their slender, coffee-coloured stalks and long writhing tentacles giving them a hair style that Medusa might well have envied. Every rock was encrusted with pink, white or green coral, fine forests of minute sea-weeds including a delicate growth of *Acetabularia mediterranea* with slender thread-like stalks and perched on the top of each stalk something that looked like a small green parasol turned inside out by some submarine wind. Occasionally a rock would be encrusted with a great black lump of sponge covered with gaping, protuberant mouths like miniature volcanoes. You could pull these sponges off the rocks and split them open with a razor blade, for sometimes, inside, you would find curious forms of life; but the sponge, in retaliation, would coat your hands with a mucus that smelt horribly of stale garlic and took hours to wear off. Scattered along the shore and in the rock pools, I would find new shells to add to my collection and half the delight of collecting these was not only the beautiful shapes of the shells themselves, but the extraordinarily evocative names that had been given to them. A pointed shell like a large winkle, the lip of whose mouth had been elongated into a series of semi-webbed fingers, was, I discovered to my delight, called the Pelican's Foot. An almost circular white, conical limpet-like shell went under the name of Chinaman's Hat. Then there were the Ark Shells and the two sides of these strange box-like shells, when separated, did look (if one used a modicum of imagination) like the hulks of two little arks. Then there were the Tower Shells, twisted and pointed as a Narwhal's horn and the Top Shells, gaily striped with a zigzag pattern of scarlet, black or blue. Under some of the bigger rocks, you would find Key-hole Limpets, each one of which had, as the name implied, a strange key-hole like aperture in the top of the shell, through which the creature breathed. And then, best of all, if you were lucky, you would find the flattened Ormers, scaly grey with a row of holes along one side, but if you turned it over and extracted its rightful occupant, you would find the whole interior of the shell glowing in opalescent, sunset colours, magical in their beauty. I had at that time no aquarium, so I was forced to construct for myself, in one corner of the bay, a rock pool some eight feet long by four feet wide, and into this I would put my various captures so that I could be almost certain of knowing where they would be on the following day.

It was in this bay that I caught my first spider crab. I would have walked right past him thinking him to be a weed-covered rock, if he had not made an incautious movement. His body was about the size and shape of a small flattened pear and at the pointed end it was decorated with a series of spikes, ending in two horn-like protuberances over his eyes. His legs and his pincers were long, slender and spindly. But the thing that intrigued me most was the fact that he was wearing, on his back and on his legs, a complete suit of tiny sea-weeds, which appeared to be growing out of his shell. Enchanted by this weird creature, I carried him triumphantly along the beach to my rock pool and placed him in it. The firm grip with which I had had to hold him (for once having discovered that he was recognized as a crab he made desperate efforts to escape) had rubbed off quite a lot of his sea-weed suit by the time I got him to the pool. I placed him in the shallow, clear water and, lying on my stomach, watched him to see what he would do. Standing high on his toes, like a spider in a hurry, he scuttled a foot or so away from where I had put him and then froze. He sat like this for a long time, so long in fact that I was just deciding that he was going to remain immobile for the rest of the morning, recovering from the shock of capture, when he suddenly extended a long, delicate claw and very daintily, almost shyly, plucked a tiny piece of sea-weed which was growing on a nearby rock. He put the sea-weed to his mouth and I could see him mumbling at it. At first I thought he was eating it, but I soon realized I was mistaken for, with angular grace, he placed his claw over his back, felt around in a rather fumbling sort of way, and then planted the tiny piece of weed on his carapace. I presumed that he had been making the base of the weed sticky with saliva or some similar substance to make it adhere to his back. As I watched him, he trundled slowly round the pool collecting a variety of sea-weed with the assiduous dedication of a professional botanist in a hitherto unexplored jungle. Within an hour or so his back was covered with such a thick layer of growth that, if he sat still and I took my eyes off him for a moment, I had difficulty in knowing exactly where he was.

Intrigued by this cunning form of camouflage, I searched the bay carefully until I found another spider crab. For him I built a special small pool with a sandy floor, completely devoid of weed. I put him in and he settled down quite happily. The following day I returned, carrying with me a nail brush (which turned out to be Larry's) and, taking the unfortunate spider crab, scrubbed him vigorously until not an atom of weed remained on his back or legs. Then I dropped into his pool a variety of things; a number of tiny top shells and some broken fragments of coral, some small sea anemones and some minute bits of bottle glass which had been sandpapered by the sea so that they looked like misty jewels. Then I sat down to watch.

The crab, when returned to his pool, sat quite still for several minutes, obviously recovering from the indignity of the scrubbing I had given him. Then, as if he could not quite believe the terrible fate that had overtaken him, he put his two pincers over his head and felt his back with the utmost delicacy, presumably hoping against hope that at least one frond of sea-weed remained. But I had done my task well and his back was shining and bare. He walked a few paces tentatively and then squatted down and sulked for half an hour. Then he roused himself out of his gloom, walked over to the edge of the pond and tried to wedge himself under a dark ridge of rock. There he sat brooding miserably over his lack of camouflage until it was time for me to go home.

I returned very early the following morning and, to my delight, saw that the crab had been busy while I had been away. Making the best of a bad job, he had decorated the top of his shell with a number of the ingredients that I had left for him. He looked extremely gaudy and had an air of carnival about him. Striped top shells had been pasted on, interspersed with bits of coral and up near his head he was wearing two beadlet anemones, like an extremely saucy bonnet with ribbons. I thought, as I watched him crawling about the sand, that he looked exceedingly conspicuous, but, curiously enough, when he went over and squatted by his favourite overhang of rock, he turned into what appeared to be a little pile of shell and coral debris, with a couple of anemones perched on top of it.

PAULA FOX

The Strength of Life

from *One-Eyed Cat*

Ned Wallis, the only son of a country clergy-
man and his young invalid wife, lived a quiet
life, ruffled only by their moody housekeeper,
Mrs Scallop. That is, until he was given a
surprising present for his eleventh birthday.

Reverend Wallis disapproved of the gleaming
new air-rifle and put it away in the attic. But
Ned was drawn towards it like a magnet, and
when he crept out in the dead of night, he shot
at a moving target . . .

What followed was like a bad dream. Ned
found a wild cat with one eye shot away, and
couldn't stop thinking about it. His school
friends, Billy, Janet and Evelyn, wouldn't have
understood his feelings. His mother sensed
something was wrong, but Ned was silenced by
his secret guilt.

When the winter set in, Ned watched over
the wild cat fearfully with the help of his
neighbour, old Mr Scully.

This story is set in the state of New York
some years ago . . .

Ned LOVED SNOW, the whisper when he walked
through it, a sound like candles being blown out,
the coming indoors out of it into the warmth, and
standing on the register in the big hall through which the
dusty, metal-smelling heat blew up, and the going back out
again, shivering, cold, stooping and scooping up a handful
to make a snowball, packing it hard with wet mittens,
hefting it, tossing it as far as he could, and the runners of his
sled whispering across it as he sleighed down the slopes
which were smooth and glittering and hard, like great
jewels.

On the first of December, there was a heavy snowfall.
When Ned looked out of his window the next morning, the
river glowed like a snake made out of light as it wound
among the snow-covered mountains.

He ate breakfast hastily, too preoccupied to read the story
on the cereal box. Mrs Scallop was broody this morning and
left him alone, her glance passing over him as it passed over
the kitchen chairs.

On the porch, he paused to take deep breaths of air which tasted, he imagined, like water from the centre of the ocean, then he waded into the snow, passing the Packard, its windows white and hidden, the crab-apple tree with its weighted branches, down the long hill trying to guess if he was anywhere near the buried driveway. By the time he reached Mr Scully's house, his galoshes were topped with snow and his feet were wet. Mr Scully's shades were drawn; the house had a pinched look as though it felt the cold.

Ned went around to the back until he could see the shed. There were boot tracks in the snow leading to it and returning to the back door. He guessed the old man had taken in the cat's bowl; it was nowhere to be seen. You couldn't leave anything out in this weather, it would freeze. Mr Scully had told him that finding water in the winter was a big problem for animals. Licking the snow or ice could make them sick.

Ned stared hard at the shed. Perhaps the cat was inside, squeezed in behind the logs in a tight space where its own breath would keep it warm. He was going to be late to school if he didn't get a move on, but he kept looking hard all over the yard as though he could make the cat appear out of snow and grey sky. Twice, his glance passed over the refrigerator. The third time, he saw the motionless mound on top of it was not only the quilt but the cat, joined into one shape by a dusting of snow.

Ned held his breath for a moment, then put his own feet in Mr Scully's tracks and went towards the shed. The tracks had frozen and they crunched under Ned's weight, but the cat didn't raise its head. Ned halted a few feet away from it – but of course, he realized, it wouldn't hear him because of its deaf ear. He could have gone closer to it than he'd ever been but he had a sudden vision of the cat exploding into fear when it finally did hear him.

When he got back to the front of the house, he saw fresh footsteps on the road. He could tell it was the road because of the deep ditches which fell away to either side. He guessed they were Billy's tracks. It was odd to think that

Billy, huffing and puffing, had gone past Mr Scully's place, thinking his own thoughts, while he, Ned, only a few yards away, had been searching for the cat. He found Evelyn's tracks too, and later on, Janet's, the smallest of all. He felt ghostly as if he'd been left alone on a white, silent globe.

Somewhere in the evergreen woods, snow must have slid off a bough, for he heard the loud plop, then the fainter sound of the bough springing up, relieved of the weight. He thought about the cat, visualizing how it had looked on the quilt. How still it had been! Why hadn't he gone right up to it, looked at it close, touched its fur? Why had it been so motionless – still as death, still as a dead vole he'd seen last summer in the grass near the well? He came to the snow-covered blacktop road upon which a few cars had left their ridged tyre tracks. He had a strong impulse to turn back, to play truant for the first time in his life. Mr Scully, with his poor eyesight, might not spot the cat on top of the refrigerator, might not, then, set food out for it. Fretting and shivering, his feet numb, Ned went on to school.

He tried very hard to concentrate on his lessons, to watch Miss Jefferson's plump, even handwriting on the blackboard as she wrote out the lines from a poem by Thomas Gray that the class was to memorize that week, but try as he might, the image of the unmoving animal on the ragged old quilt persisted. Last week, on a rainy afternoon, the cat had looked at Ned, had cocked its head as though to see him better. Its one eye, narrowed, had reminded him of a grain of wheat.

> The curfew tolls the knell of parting day,
> The lowing herd wind slowly o'er the lea . . .

Ned read the lines several times before copying them down in his copybook. The words made no sense to him. It was this that had made his hours in school so hard ever since he and Mr Scully had seen the cat last autumn, this drawing away of his attention from everything that was going on around him. He was either relieved because the cat was where he could see it or fearful because he didn't know where it was.

In the afternoon, on the way home, Ned got into a fight with Billy.

Janet stumbled over a hidden root as she turned up her path. She fell forward, dropping her books. Ned picked them up, brushed off the snow and handed them to her as she got to her feet.

'Goody-goody!' shouted Billy. 'Mama's goody boy!'

Ned felt a fierce single impulse. His arm swung out like a chain of lead, and he knocked Billy into the snow with a triumphant howl of joy. Janet's mouth fell open in astonishment.

It was the deep frozen end of late afternoon, and the snow had hardened. He and Billy rolled about on it, grabbing at each other's ears and faces.

'Stop that!' Evelyn shouted.

'Oh, you boys! How I hate boys!' cried Janet.

Ned and Billy got to their feet. Billy's knitted hat was still on. Ned found himself hating it for its silliness – it stood up so high on top of Billy's great round head. All at once, Billy stuck out his tongue. Ned burst into laughter, and in a moment Billy was laughing, too. Evelyn gave them a disgusted look and trudged on ahead, but Janet paused, looking puzzled, and asked Billy if he *liked* to be knocked down. He only grinned at her.

For the first time in a while, Ned felt like himself, or what he thought of as himself. He and Billy walked along companionably all the way to Mr Scully's house, talking about hockey, and how the pond near school must be frozen solid by now and maybe the bigger boys would let them skate around the edges of the game this year. Ned remembered how the boys had skated, holding their hockey sticks diagonally across themselves, how their racing skates flashed against the cracked, milky ice, how they'd shouted at Billy and him to stay out of their way, how they'd looked like warriors.

Billy went on home and Ned slid most of the way down to

the state road to Mr Scully's mailbox. There was no newspaper today; he guessed the snow must have stopped the
delivery boy. But there was a handwritten note that said the
new garage down the state road would be finished pretty
soon. Mr Scully's Ford banger was practically buried by the
snow. Ned guessed Papa would pick up Mr Scully's
groceries for him, just as he'd done in the past when the
weather was bad and Mr Scully was afraid the banger would
get stuck in a ditch somewhere.

His chin was freezing; he held his mitten over it, thinking how good a cup of hot tea would taste as he clambered
up towards the house. He pulled himself over a patch of ice
by grabbing on to the shingles of the outhouse. He looked
over at the refrigerator just under the shed roof. The cat was
lying on the quilt just as he had last seen it in the morning.
He groaned out loud. He glanced towards the house. Mr
Scully was staring out the kitchen window at the cat.

Ned ran, stumbling and slipping, to the back door. Mr
Scully took a hundred years to open it.

'Is he dead? Is the cat dead?' cried Ned.

'Come in. Come inside, quick! Don't let the cold in.'

Ned leaned against the kitchen table. The snow melted
off his galoshes and made a little pool on the floor. He kept
his eyes on Mr Scully's face.

'Take your wet things off, Ned,' the old man said quietly.
'No, at least, he isn't dead yet. Right after you went home
yesterday, I saw him scrabble up there on his quilt. He
settled down and seemed all right. But when I set out his
supper for him, he didn't pay attention like he usually does.
It began to snow and I didn't know what to do. I didn't want
to chance grabbing and putting him way inside the shed.
Those wild ones can hurt you. And I thought maybe it
would scare him if I tried that – he's such a timid fellow. I
kept an eye on him and the snow got deeper and he didn't
move. I went to bed finally. I told you how bad I sleep, Ned.
Old people don't sleep the way young people do, they wake
up so easy. Maybe it was the snow stopping that got me up. I
came downstairs with my candle and set it down here on

the table. I thought to have a cup of tea. Take off your coat, Ned. Put it over the chair there by the stove. One of the few nice things about age is you can give in to yourself in little ways. I wouldn't have dreamed of drinking a cup of tea in the middle of the night when I was young. Who ever heard of such a thing?'

Ned couldn't shake his head or smile or say a word.

'Calm down,' Mr Scully said. 'The cat's sick. That's what I'm explaining to you. Anyhow, I looked out in the yard. I could just make him out, you know, because the sky was all cleared out of snow. So I put on my coat and my boots and went out to the refrigerator and stood right next to him. At first I thought he was dead, that he'd climbed up there to die. After a while, though, I heard him breathing, just a little whisper of air being taken in and let out. In fact, I even rested my hand on his neck and he let out a sound – poor devil, it wasn't purring – like a piece of glass scratching a stone. I guess his throat's hurt, too. I put his bowl of food right on the quilt beside him. He lifted his head a touch and looked at it out of his eye. But he didn't want it. His head sank down again so I brought the bowl back in. It would have frozen. Since then I've taken him food several times. He don't bother to even look now.'

'Is he dying because of what happened to his eye?' Ned asked in a choked voice.

'I don't think that. People put rat poison in their barns to kill the vermin. He might have eaten some. Anything can happen. Is that a letter in your hand?'

Ned handed him the notice about the new garage. 'Pooh!' exclaimed the old man, crumpling it and putting it into the stove. Ned put his coat back on and walked out of the kitchen. Mr Scully didn't say a word to stop him.

During the time he'd been inside the feeling of the day had changed. It now held the silence of midnight, a kind of silence Ned had listened to when he'd awakened with a sore throat, or a pain in his stomach from eating too much dessert.

He walked to the refrigerator, stamping heavily on the

snow as he went. The cat didn't move. Ned drew closer. He gripped the refrigerator and peered up at the cat. He stretched one hand over its back. The closer he lowered his hand to it, the more he felt it was alive, even if it was barely alive. There was a breath of difference; he seemed to feel it in his fingers.

'You could tell, couldn't you?' asked Mr Scully when Ned returned to the kitchen. 'It's funny but you can always tell.'

'He'll freeze to death,' Ned said.

'You can't know that for sure. If the temperature doesn't drop too much further, he might make it. I'd let him come in here, but he won't do it. I've held the door open for him. He runs away.'

It was brave of Mr Scully, Ned thought, to have offered the cat the shelter of the house.

'Well, yes,' the old man said, as though Ned had actually remarked on his bravery. 'I did try – thinking about the hard weather coming up and him being in poor shape for hunting. But he seemed to be getting so strong. Ever since we watched him playing, I believed he might have a real chance. Here's your tea. Let's sit by the stove. Then I'd appreciate it if you'd fetch down one last box from the attic. I know it's there because it's not in the parlour. Once we've gone through it, the whole place will be in order. In as much order as I can manage.'

Ned drank his tea. It warmed him and comforted him; for a little while he stopped thinking about the grey mound on the quilt. He went up a little ladder to the hole that let him into the attic and found the last object it held. It wasn't a box but a leather satchel, one strap holding it together, the leather nearly rotted away. There was nothing left in the dark space but cobwebs and old planks with rusty nails poking through them.

He brought the satchel to the kitchen table, and Mr Scully unbuckled the strap carefully.

'Look at that . . .' he said wonderingly. The satchel was filled with a child's clothing. A blackened spoon with a curved handle fell on the table. The old man rubbed it with his finger and the tarnish came off. 'Silver,' he said softly. 'What Doris ate her cereal with . . .' There were high-buttoned shoes that had once been white and were now the colour of curds. Mr Scully held up a sprigged cotton dress with a crocheted collar that crumbled in his hand. 'She wore that to a birthday party when we lived in Pough-keepsie. My, my . . . think of her, way out in the golden west.' He stared at Ned for a minute, then shook his head as though saying *no* to something. 'I must throw this all away. There's no use for it now.'

Ned washed their cups and piled up a few sticks of wood near the stove. He put on his coat. Mr Scully said, 'Ned, wait . . .' Ned paused at the door. Mr Scully stared at him. Then he said, 'While you were up in the attic, I looked at the cat. I'm pretty sure he lifted up his head.'

As Ned walked home the dark set in. He was cold and tired, and fear for the cat's life tugged at him. Then he saw the lights shining through the windows of his home; he thought of the voices of his parents, and the echo of their voices that seemed to fill the rooms and halls of the house even when they were silent, Papa working in his study and Mama reading in her wheelchair.

He glanced through the bay windows of the living room and saw the pussywillow wallpaper his grandmother had chosen, the top of the bronze lion's back, the parchment shade of the lamp his father read the newspaper by. The room was empty. For a brief moment, he felt years had passed since he'd left for school that morning. He ran quickly to the front and up the porch steps, opened the door with a wrench and ran into the hall.

His father's coat hung from the coat stand, its hem falling on the handles of two umbrellas no one ever used. On the table where his father often left his old leather briefcase – and sometimes a box of chocolates he bought in Waterville – he saw an envelope addressed to him. It was the first letter Uncle Hilary had ever mailed directly to him. He opened it and read it:

Dear Ned,

On our way south, we may stop off to visit an island I've recently learned about where there are small wild ponies which live in a forest. Presumably, a ferryboat delivers mail and supplies to the island, so we'll just grab a ride on it. Be sure to pack books. I'll telephone from New York City as soon as I've made all our arrangements. I am only sorry you don't have a year's vacation instead of ten days. But, of course, a person only has a year's vacation before the age of five.

Ned realized with a start that Christmas was only a few weeks away. He was standing there with his coat still on, wondering what could save him from this vacation trip which he now dreaded nearly as much as if it were to be spent alone with Mrs Scallop, when she appeared, her finger to her lips, walking towards him. Since he rarely said more than hello to her, he couldn't imagine why she was warning him to be silent.

'You must be very quiet,' she said in a loud whisper. 'Your mother is very ill.'

Ned tore off his coat, flung it at the coat stand and started for the stairs.

As he put his foot on the first step, he heard a trembling sign that was nearly a word float down from above. He stopped, frightened. He turned hesitantly to Mrs Scallop. She was nodding as though satisfied.

Then he took the stairs two at a time, going up fast because he didn't want to go up at all. He heard a second sigh, somewhat fainter. He reached the top of the stairs and saw his father bending over his mother's bed. His father looked up, saw him, and glanced down at the bed, then walked quickly out of the room to Ned.

'She's been suffering,' Papa said in a low voice. 'The pain has diminished, but she's quite weak. You'd best not go in right now, Neddy. You go and have your supper. I'll sit with her until she falls asleep.'

Ned ate at the kitchen table, watched over closely by Mrs

Scallop, whose lips moved faintly each time he picked up a pea with his fork. She had made chocolate pudding, which was nearly his favourite dessert: He took no pleasure in it, his mind either on his mother or the cat. Mrs Scallop noticed he wasn't eating and said, 'Mrs Scallop is known for her chocolate pudding, yet Neddy is so ungrateful for such a great treat that he simply fiddles with that wonderful pudding on his spoon!'

'What do you care whether I eat or not?' he suddenly cried out at her.

He had never spoken back to any grown-up before, and he was astonished at himself. Mrs Scallop stared at him, her thin lower lip pushed out like a child pouting. 'How could you raise your voice to me?' she asked in a tiny voice, as though her throat had shrunk to the size of a pin. To Ned's dismay, a large tear appeared on the lower lid of her right eye. One tear, he observed to himself, despite his embarrassment – how can a person cry one tear from one eye?

He got up so hurriedly, he knocked the chair down. Picking it up, he muttered an apology. She hadn't moved. The tear travelled slowly down her large cheek. He had to go right upstairs to do his homework, he said, and he wasn't hungry tonight but he thanked her for the pudding. He was gripping the back of the chair so hard he heard the wood creak.

'Well, I *do* care what you eat,' Mrs Scallop said in a child's voice.

'Oh, I know you do,' Ned said, and realized he had sounded just like Papa. Clumsily, half-bowing, he managed to get out of the kitchen.

At the top of the stairs, he saw a small lamp had been lit in his mother's room and placed near the windows. His father was asleep in the chair by the bed. Ned leaned around the doorway and saw Mama, her face white against the pillow, her eyes wide open. She turned her head slightly and stared up at him. She put a finger to her lips, as Mrs Scallop had done, and pointed to Papa. She smiled faintly at him, and Ned tried to smile back.

He went to his own room. What a day it had been! The best part of it had been fighting, then making up, with Billy. He was almost happy when he shut the door and turned on the light and saw his books on their shelf, his yellow-painted dresser. He went and sat in the small woven chair Uncle Hilary had brought him from the Philippine Islands years ago. He could barely fit in it. For a long time, he sat in the chair and watched the lights twinkle across the river, glad to be away from the pain and craziness of grown-ups.

Later, when he crawled under his blanket, he found he couldn't sleep. He thought for a moment of taking one of his late-night walks through the house, but he suddenly recalled the rather strange emptiness of the living room when he'd looked through the windows after coming home from Mr Scully's. It wasn't only that no one had been in the room. It was as though the whole house had been empty.

The cold didn't abate for several days, and Ned and Mr Scully spent a good deal of time at the kitchen window watching the cat. It continued to raise its head now and then, and each time it did so, Ned and the old man would exclaim and one or the other would remark that it was still alive. They took turns taking out bowls of food. Once, Ned pushed the bowl right up to the cat's face and it made a sound. 'It's like a rusty key turning in a lock,' he reported to Mr Scully.

'It wants to be let alone,' Mr Scully said resolutely. 'And that's what we must do now, Ned, leave it alone.'

'Couldn't we take him to a doctor?'

'I don't believe a doctor could get near him. Weak as he is, when I touched his head this afternoon before you got here, he hissed at me and opened his jaws. Let me tell you, Ned, he's a wild cat. We must wait and be patient and see. Anyhow, I haven't the money to pay an animal doctor.'

The next day, Mr Scully and Ned concluded the cat was dead. There had been a brief snow flurry in the afternoon, and the animal was covered with a layer of snow. Mr Scully had been unable to detect any breathing.

'Come away from the window, Ned. You'll wear a hole in the glass. If the cat's dead, I'll dispose of it tomorrow. I'm worried about a few things I want to talk to you about.'

Reluctantly, Ned dragged himself from the window and sat down across from Mr Scully at the kitchen table.

'It's the stovepipe,' said the old man. His voice had risen and his skin had a mottled, bruised look. Ned realized he was agitated.

'There's a host of things that need doing,' Mr Scully went on, speaking quickly. 'That stovepipe has to be cleaned out or I'll burn the house down around my head. I've written to Doris and I'd be obliged if you gave the letter to the Reverend and had him mail it. I'll give you the two pennies for the stamp. Winter is such a hard time! Just a few degrees difference in the temperature and look what happens!'

The old man's voice, its exasperated tone, showed Ned that he was tired of the cat. His heart sank. It was as if the cat weighed two hundred pounds and now he would have to carry it alone.

He took Mr Scully's letter to Doris home with him and gave it to his father along with the two pennies for the stamp. When he went upstairs, he saw that his mother was dressed and in her wheelchair for the first time since her attack on the day of his fight with Billy. She looked pale, but as soon as she saw him, she smiled and told him to come in. One of her hands was gripped around her favourite china cup that was painted with rosebuds and rose leaves and was so thin you could see through it when you held it up to a light.

'Don't look so worried, Neddy. I'm much better,' she said.

He went to her, and she took her hand from the cup and put it on his. The swelling of her joints had lessened. He knew that that was what she had wanted him to see.

'It's mysterious,' she said. 'What makes it worse or better, no one seems to know. It's like sailing a small boat through reefs – you never know what you're going to hit or when. I'm tired, but that's all. I almost think I could walk.

It's been a while since I tried. My legs are pretty weak, yet I think I could.'

Slowly she extended one foot from beneath the blanket which covered her knees and lap.

'Uncle Hilary brought you those slippers from China,' Ned said.

'He brings us the world, doesn't he? Aren't you glad to be going on a trip with him?'

It was hard to lie to her. Instead of answering her question, he said he had to run back to Mr Scully's. He'd forgotten to bring in a second load of wood for the stove, and it was so cold, Mr Scully might need it.

He ran downstairs and put on his coat and went outside to stand shivering under the crab-apple tree on the north side of the house. As he looked up at the stained-glass window on the staircase landing, he knew he'd never been quite so miserable in his life. Through the kitchen window, he saw Mrs Scallop standing at the sink. She seemed to be singing. Suddenly she flung out both her arms as though conducting an orchestra. She held a potato in one hand and a carrot in the other. In the middle of feeling so terrible, Ned found himself laughing. He could not have believed, until that moment, that Mrs Scallop would ever be able to make him feel better – but she had.

He got up early the next day, Saturday, and started out for Mr Scully's house without stopping for breakfast.

The weather had changed. The sky was clear, and Ned walked down the slope in the pale yellow winter sunlight. From the meadows rose the rustling sound of ice and snow thawing.

Ned stamped the snow from his boots and went into the kitchen. Mr Scully was looking out the window. He turned to Ned, every tooth in his jaw visible as his mouth widened in an immense smile.

'He wasn't dead at all!' he shouted at Ned even though he was standing only a foot or two away from him. 'The old fellow's gone! Look out there. He got up and went. I can see his paw prints over there under the pine tree branch. See?

Whatever it was – poison, germs – he wore it out! Now he's off to take care of things. He hung on. I'd given up – but he fooled me! Isn't that wonderful? To be fooled like that?'

Ned was dazed. Happiness came like a strong blow across his back, and it smelled of the fresh coffee Mr Scully had made for himself and of wood smoke, and it was the buttery colour of the ray of sun across the kitchen table, and the colour, too, of the blackened quilt, no longer a bed for a dying animal.

He heard the Packard go by and wished he was sitting in it with Papa. He could have gone to church with him today after all, if he'd known about the cat. Papa would be meeting with the deacons about the Christmas programmes, and the Ladies Aid Society would be in the basement stringing cranberry and popcorn balls for the Christmas tree, and candying apples, and wrapping presents for the children of the congregation. And it might even be today that the great church doors would be opened and half a dozen men would carry in the enormous tree. One person would go up to the gallery and put the big star in place, then the rest of the tree would be decorated. And Christmas Eve the tree would fill the entire church with its marvellous smell of deep pine woods and snow, and there would be, too, the peppermint smell of candy canes. But he wouldn't be there! He would be on his way to Charleston with Uncle Hilary.

Mr Scully was telling him that he felt so cheered up, he thought he'd smoke a bit of tobacco, although it had probably dried up by now and wouldn't be worth lighting. His pipe was in the parlour, and when he went to get it, opening the door wide, Ned smelled the cold apple-scented air. Mr Scully kept his baskets of apples in the parlour, along with a sack each of potatoes and onions. Mr Scully came back to the kitchen with his meerschaum, which had a collie dog carved in amber on the bowl. The old man looked stronger to Ned than he had for a long time, and he was moving quickly as he filled up the pipe bowl and tamped down the tobacco, got a match from the tin box on the windowsill, and struck it alight.

'He'll come back and I'll feed him,' said Mr Scully. 'He'll be hungry now, and he'll want to get his strength back. Mrs Kimball brought me a chicken yesterday. I'll give him some of that. You'll see . . . We'll have him running around soon.'

'You're glad, too,' Ned said, surprised. He had thought the old man was just being patient with him, putting up with Ned's concern about the cat. Now he could see Mr Scully felt responsible – more than that, sympathetic – towards the animal.

'I'm glad,' Mr Scully said in a serious voice. 'When you get to be my age, the strength of life in a living creature can't help but gladden your heart. I don't know the reason for that, but there it is.'

Mrs Scallop was somewhere upstairs when Ned got home so he was able to make his own breakfast and eat it alone in the kitchen. He washed his dishes and put them away, then he went upstairs to his mother's room.

'I am glad I'm going away with Uncle Hilary,' he said to her.

She laughed, and said, 'Why, yes! That is an answer to what I asked you yesterday, isn't it? Sometimes it takes you a while to answer a question.'

He couldn't tell her all that had happened since yesterday, and why he felt so much better.

'I have some news. Your Papa has driven Mrs Scallop to Waterville this morning. He's found work for her in a nursing home for old people. You remember how we talked about her needing a small country of her own? She may get one. Papa has taken her to her interview. She was wearing a hat that looked like a pumpkin pie. It may have been, for that matter. In any case, I'm sure it will impress the people who will hire her.'

'How did Papa tell her that she wasn't to stay with us any more?'

She laughed again. 'We had to rehearse it all,' she said. 'He didn't want to lie, of course. But he had to dress up the truth a tiny bit. He told her we were thinking seriously of moving to the parsonage, and that we really needed a practical nurse to watch over me until we moved. I'm so happy she's leaving.' Mama sighed and looked out of her windows. 'What a glorious day! I like that mildness that can come in the middle of winter. Well, she was efficient, I'll give her that. But I do believe she disliked me immensely because I didn't admire the heart on her sleeve enough. In fact, her real heart, I suspect, may look like one of those rugs she makes.'

Ned felt Mama was really speaking to herself. She was still looking out of the window; her voice was dreamy.

'Is there really going to be a practical nurse?' he asked.

She turned now and smiled at him as though suddenly seeing him standing there, his hand on the wheelchair arm.

'Yes, and it's Mrs Kimball.'

'Evelyn's mother?'

'Indeed, yes. The newest baby, Patrick, Junior, is on a bottle now, so that one of the other children can look after him. Your Papa spoke to her several weeks ago – it works out well for us all.'

'Everything is happening,' Ned said.

'It always is,' said Mama.

JULIUS LESTER

The Man Who Was a Horse

from *Long Journey Home*

It sounds strange, doesn't it? How can a man also be a horse? What allows Bob Lemmons to 'become' a horse in this true story is his gentleness, his patience, his lack of fear. With these qualities he is stronger than all the other cowboys put together, and he knows the joy of riding as one with a herd of wild mustang horses: proud and free . . .

IT WASN'T NOON YET, but the sun had already made the Texas plains hotter than an oven. Bob Lemmons pulled his wide-brimmed hat tighter to his head and rode slowly away from the ranch.

'Good luck, Bob!' someone yelled.

Bob didn't respond. His mind was already on the weeks ahead. He walked his horse slowly, being in no particular hurry. That was one thing he had learned early. One didn't capture a herd of mustang horses in a hurry. For all he knew, a mustang stallion might have been watching him at that very moment, and if he were galloping, the stallion might get suspicious and take the herd miles away.

Bob looked around him, and as far as he could see the land was flat, stretching unbroken like the cloudless sky over his head until the two seemed to meet. Nothing appeared to be moving except him on his horse, but he knew that a herd of mustangs could be galloping near the horizon line at that moment and he would be unable to see it until it came much closer.

The Man Who Was a Horse

He rode north that day, seeing no sign of mustangs until close to evening, when he came across some tracks. He stopped and dismounted. For a long while he stared at the tracks until he was able to identify several of the horses. As far as he could determine, it seemed to be a small herd of a stallion, seven or eight mares, and a couple of colts. The tracks were no more than three days old and he half expected to come in sight of the herd the next day or two. A herd didn't travel in a straight line, but ranged back and forth within what the stallion considered his territory. Of course, that could be the size of a county. But Bob knew he was in it, though he had not seen a horse.

He untied his blanket from behind the saddle and laid it out on the ground. Then he removed the saddle from the horse and hobbled the animal to a stake. He didn't want a mustang stallion coming by during the night and stealing his horse. Stallions were good at that. Many times he had known them to see a herd of tame horses and, for who knew what reason, become attracted to one mare and cut her out of the herd.

He took his supper out of the saddlebags and ate slowly as the chilly night air seemed to rise from the very plains that a few short hours before had been too hot for a man to walk on. He threw the blanket around his shoulders, wishing he could make a fire. But if he had, the smell of woodsmoke in his clothes would have been detected by any herd he got close to.

After eating he laid his head back against his saddle and covered himself with his thick Mexican blanket. The chilliness of the night made the stars look to him like shining slivers of ice. Someone had once told him that the stars were balls of fire, like the sun, but Bob didn't feel them that way. But he wasn't educated, so he wouldn't dispute with anybody about it. Just because you gave something a name didn't mean that that was what it actually was, though. The thing didn't know it had that name, so it just kept on being what it was. And as far as he was concerned, people would be better off if they tried to know a thing like it knew itself. That was the only way he could ever explain to somebody how he was able to bring in a herd of wild horses by himself. The way other people did it was to go out in groups of two and three and run a herd until it almost dropped from exhaustion. He guessed that was all right. It worked. But he couldn't do it that way. He knew he wouldn't want anybody running him to and fro for days on end, until he hardly knew up from down or left from right.

Even while he was still a slave, he'd felt that way about mustangs. Other horses too. But he had never known anything except horses. Born and raised on a ranch, he had legally been a slave until 1865, when the slaves in Texas were freed. He had been eighteen at the time and hadn't understood when Mr Hunter had come and told him that he was free. That was another one of those words, Bob thought. Even as a child, when his father told him he was a slave, he'd wondered what he meant. What did a slave look like? What did a slave feel like? He didn't think he had ever known. He and his parents had been the only coloured people on the ranch and he guessed it wasn't until after he was 'freed' that he saw another coloured person. He knew sometimes, from the names he heard the cowboys use, that his colour somehow made him different. He heard them talking about 'fighting a war over the nigger', but it meant nothing to him. So when Mr Hunter had told him he was free, that he could go wherever he wanted to, he nodded and got on his horse and went on out to the range to see after the cattle like he was supposed to. He smiled to himself, wondering how Mr Hunter had ever gotten the notion that he couldn't have gone where he wanted.

A few months after that he brought in his first herd of mustangs. He had been seeing the wild horses since he could remember. The first time had been at dusk one day. He had been playing near the corral when he happened to look towards the mesa and there, standing atop it, was a lone stallion. The wind blew against it and its mane and tail flowed in the breeze like tiny ribbons. The horse stood there for a long while; then without warning, it suddenly wheeled and galloped away. Even now Bob remembered how seeing the horse had been like looking into a mirror. He'd never told anyone that, sensing that they would perhaps think him a little touched in the head. Many people thought it odd enough that he could bring in a herd of mustangs by himself. But after that, whenever he saw one mustang or a herd, he felt like he was looking at himself.

One day several of the cowboys went out to capture a herd. The ranch was short of horses and no one ever thought of buying horses when there were so many wild ones. He had wanted to tell them that he would bring in the horses, but they would have laughed at him. Who'd ever heard of one man bringing in a herd? So he watched them ride out, saying nothing. A few days later they were back, tired and disgusted. They hadn't even been able to get close to a herd.

That evening Bob timidly suggested to Mr Hunter that he be allowed to try. Everyone laughed. Bob reminded them that no one on the ranch could handle a horse like he could; that the horses came to him more than anyone else. The cowboys acknowledged that that was true, but it was impossible for one man to capture a herd. Bob said nothing else. Early the next morning he rode out alone, asking the cook to leave food in a saddlebag for him on the fence at the north pasture every day. Three weeks later the cowboys were sitting around the corral one evening and looked up to see a herd of mustangs galloping towards them, led by Bob. Despite their amazement, they moved quickly to open the gate and Bob led the horses in.

That had been some twenty years ago, and long after Bob left the Hunter Ranch he found that everywhere he went he was known. He never had trouble getting a job, but capturing mustangs was only a small part of what he did. Basically he was just a cowboy who worked from sunrise to sunset, building fences, herding cattle, branding calves, pitching hay, and doing everything else that needed to be done.

Most cowboys had married and settled down by the time

they reached his age, but Bob had long ago relinquished any such dream. Once he'd been in love with a Mexican girl, but her father didn't want her to marry a 'nigger'. Bob had been as confused as ever at being labelled that. He would never know what that word meant to old José. But whatever it was, it was more than enough for him to stop Pilár from marrying Bob. After that he decided not to be in love again. It wasn't a decision he'd ever regretted. Almost every morning when he got up and looked at the sky lying full and open and blue, stretching towards for ever, he knew he was married to something. He wanted to say the sky, but it was more than that. He wanted to say everything, but he felt that it was more than that, too. How could there be more than everything? He didn't know, but there was.

The sun awakened him even before the first arc of its roundness showed over the horizon. He saddled his horse and rode off, following the tracks he had discovered the previous evening. He followed them west until he was certain they were leading him to the Pecos River. He smiled. Unless it was a herd travelling through, they would come to that river to drink every day. Mustangs never went too far from water, though they could go for days without a drop if necessary. The Pecos was still some distance ahead, but he felt his horse's body quiver slightly, and she began to strain forward against his tight hold on the reins. She smelled the water.

'Sorry, honey. But that water's not for you,' he told the horse. He wheeled around and galloped back in the direction of the ranch until he came to the outermost edge of what was called the west pasture. It was still some miles from the ranch house itself, and today Bob couldn't see any cattle grazing up there.

But on the fence rail enclosing the pasture was a saddlebag filled with food. Each day one of the cowboys would bring a saddlebag of food up there and leave it for him. He transferred the food to his own saddlebags. He was hungry, but would wait until evening to eat. The food had to have time to lose its human odour, an odour that mustangs could pick out of the slightest breeze. He himself would not venture too close to the horses for another few days, not until he was certain that his own odour had become that of his horse.

He rode southward from the pasture to the banks of the Nueces River. There he dismounted, took the saddle off his horse, and let her drink her fill and wade in the stream for a while. It would be a few days before she could drink from the Pecos. The mustangs would have noticed the strange odour of horse and man together, and any good stallion would have led his mares and colts away. The success of catching mustangs, as far as Bob was concerned, was never to hurry. If necessary he would spend two weeks getting a herd accustomed to his distant presence once he was in sight of them.

He washed the dust from his face and filled his canteen. He lay down under a tree, but its shade didn't offer much relief from the heat of high noon. The day felt like it was on fire and Bob decided to stay where he was until the sun began its downward journey. He thought Texas was probably the hottest place in the world. He didn't know, not having travelled much. He had been to Oklahoma, Kansas, New Mexico, Arizona, and Wyoming on cattle drives. Of all the places, he liked Wyoming the most, because of the high mountains. He'd never seen anything so high. There were mountains in Texas, but nothing like that. Those mountains just went up and up and up until it seemed they would never stop. But they always did, with snow on the top. After a few days though he wasn't sure that he did like the mountains. Even now he wasn't sure. The mountains made him feel that he was penned in a corral, and he was used to spaces no smaller than the sky. Yet he remembered Wyoming with fondness and hoped that some year another cattle drive would take him there.

The heat had not abated much when Bob decided to go north again and pick up his trail. He would camp close to the spot where his mare had first smelled the Pecos. That was close enough for now.

In the days following, Bob moved closer to the river until one evening he saw the herd come streaming out of the hills, across the plain, and to the river. He was some distance away, but he could see the stallion lift his head and sniff the breeze. Bob waited. Although he couldn't know for sure, he could feel the stallion looking at him, and for a tense moment Bob didn't know if the horse would turn and lead the herd away. But the stallion lowered his head and began to drink and the other horses came down to the river. Bob sighed. He had been accepted.

The following day he crossed the river and picked up the herd's trail. It was not long after sunrise before he saw them grazing. He went no closer, wanting only to keep them in sight and, most important, make them feel his presence. He was glad to see that after a moment's hesitation, the stallion went back to grazing.

Bob felt sorry for the male horse. It always had to be on guard against dangers. If it relaxed for one minute, that just might be the minute a nearby panther would choose to strike, or another stallion would challenge him for the lead of the herd, or some cowboys would throw out their ropes. He wondered why a stallion wanted the responsibility. Even while the horses were grazing, Bob noticed that the stallion was separate, over to one side, keeping a constant lookout. He would tear a few mouthfuls of grass from the earth, then raise his head high, looking and smelling for danger.

At various times throughout the day Bob moved a few hundred yards closer. He could see it clearly now. The stallion was brown, the colour of the earth. The mares and colts were black and brown. No sorrels or duns in this herd. They were a little smaller than his horse. But all mustangs were. Their size, though, had nothing to do with their strength or endurance. There was no doubt that they were the best horses. He, however, had never taken one from the many herds he had brought in. It wasn't that he wouldn't have liked one. He would have, but for him to have actually ridden one would have been like taking a piece of the sky and making a blanket. To ride with them when they were wild was all right. But he didn't think any man was really worthy of riding one, even though he brought them in for that purpose.

By the sixth day he had gotten close enough to the herd that his presence didn't attract notice. The following day he moved closer until he and his mare were in the herd itself. He galloped with the herd that day, across the plain, down to the river, up into the hills. He observed the stallion closely, noting that it was a good one. The best stallions led the herd from the rear. A mare always led from the front. But it was only at the rear that a stallion could guard the herd and keep a mare from running away. The stallion ran up and down alongside the herd, biting a slow mare on the rump or ramming another who threatened to run away or to bump a third. The stallion was king, Bob thought, but he worked. It didn't look like much fun.

He continued to run with the herd a few days more. Then came the crucial moment when, slowly, he would begin to give directions of his own, to challenge the stallion in little ways until he had completely taken command of the herd and driven the stallion off. At first he would simply lead the herd in the direction away from the one the stallion wanted to go, and just before the stallion became enraged, he would put it back on course. He did this many times, getting the stallion confused as to whether or not there was a challenger in his midst. But enough days of it and the stallion gradually wore down, knowing that something was happening, but unable to understand what. When Bob was sure the herd was in his command, he merely drove the stallion away.

Now came the fun. For two weeks Bob led the herd. Unlike the stallion, he chose to lead from the front, liking the sound and feel of the wild horses so close behind. He led them to the river and watched happily as they splashed and rolled in the water. Like the stallion, however, he kept his eyes and ears alert for any sign of danger. Sometimes he would pretend he heard something when he hadn't and would lead the herd quickly away simply as a test of their responsiveness to him.

At night he stopped, unsaddled his horse, and laid out his blanket. The herd grazed around him. During all this time he never spoke a word to the horses, not knowing what effect the sound of a voice might have on them. Sometimes he wondered what his own voice sounded like and even wondered if after some period of inactivity, he would return to the ranch and find himself able only to snort and neigh, as these were the only sounds he heard. There were other sounds though, sounds that he couldn't reproduce, like the flaring nostrils of the horses when they were galloping, the dark bulging eyes, the flesh quivering and shaking. He knew that he couldn't hear any of these things – not with his ears at least. But somewhere in his body he heard every ripple of muscles and bending of bones.

The longer he was with the herd, the less he thought. His mind slowly emptied itself of anything relating to his other life and refilled with sky, plain, grass, water, and shrubs. At these times he was more aware of the full-bodied animal beneath him. His own body seemed to take on a new life and he was aware of the wind against his chest, of the taut muscles in his strong legs and the strength of his muscles in his arms, which felt to him like the forelegs of his horses. The only thing he didn't feel he had was a tail to float in the wind behind him.

Finally, when he knew that the herd would follow him anywhere it was time to take it in. It was a day he tried to keep away as long as possible. But even he began to tire of going back to the west pasture for food and sometimes having to chase a horse that had tried to run away from the herd. He had also begun to weary of sleeping under a blanket on the ground every night. So one day, almost a month after he had left, he rode back towards the ranch until he saw one of the cowhands and told him to get the corral ready. Tomorrow he was bringing them in.

The following morning he led the herd on what he imagined was the ride of their lives. Mustangs were made to run. All of his most vivid memories were of mustangs and he remembered the day he had seen a herd of what must have been at least a thousand of them galloping across the plains. The earth was a dark ripple of movement, like the swollen Nueces at floodtime. And though his herd was much smaller, they ran no less beautifully that day.

Then, towards evening, Bob led them east, galloping, galloping, across the plains. And as he led them towards the corral, he knew that no one could ever know these horses by riding on them. One had to ride with them, feeling their hooves pound and shake the earth, their bodies glistening so close by that you could see the thin straight hairs of their shining coats. He led them past the west pasture, down the slope, and just before the corral gate, he swerved to one side, letting the horses thunder inside. The cowboys leaped and shouted, but Bob didn't stay to hear their congratulations. He slowed his mare to a trot and then to a walk to cool her off. It was after dark when he returned to the ranch.

He took his horse to the stable, brushed her down, and put her in a stall for a well-earned meal of hay. Then he walked over to the corral, where the mustangs milled restlessly. He sat on the rail for a long while, looking at them. They were only horses now. Just as he was only a man.

After a while he climbed down from the fence and went into the bunkhouse to go to sleep.

Read On!

THE EARTHWORM AWARD

The Earthworm Award was set up in 1987 by Friends of the Earth to encourage and reward the writing of books that help children to enjoy and care for the Earth, and *all* its inhabitants.

Each year a winner is chosen from books of all kinds sent in by publishers in the UK. The following ten titles have been specially selected from 400 fiction and information books submitted for the award.

THE EARTHWORM TOP TEN

Where the Forest Meets the Sea
by Jeannie Baker
Winner of the Earthworm Award 1988

This mysterious book shows us how the Earth's great tropical rainforests are disappearing fast and for ever, with beautifully crafted collages made from real pieces of rainforest.

Bringing the Rain to Kapiti Plain
by Aardema and Vidal

A traditional African tale, full of rhythm and light, with words and pictures in soft, earthy colours and flowing lines.

The Sea People
by Jorg Muller and Jorg Steiner

The only difference between people on planet Earth and the greedy islanders in this story is that they have a nearby island to move to when they destroy their home. A dramatic parable with breath-taking illustrations.

Read On!

The Boy and the Swan
by Catherine Storr
Winner of the Earthworm Award 1987

A new world opens up for a lonely orphan, when he saves the life of a helpless cygnet in this haunting novel.

Conservation
by Robert Ingren and Margaret Dunkle

If you think that conservation is boring, then think again! It means life or death to many of the inhabitants of our planet. Find out some simple reasons why, in words and pictures.

Spring Clean your Planet
by Ralph Levison

Practical advice on how *you* can take action and protect the environment.

Nicky the Nature Detective
by Ulf Svedberg

Become an expert explorer like Nicky and learn how to uncover some of nature's closely kept secrets, using this illustrated handbook.

Children of the Dust
by Louise Lawrence

A powerful and gripping story of nuclear destruction and a desperate fight for survival.

Bird
by David Burnie

A pictorial encyclopaedia of bird relics, produced in conjunction with the Natural History Museum, full of fascinating data and a magnificent array of photographs.

Listening to Nature
by Joseph Cornell

A beautiful collection of writings and images of nature for thoughtful readers.

Acknowledgements

The editor and publishers gratefully acknowledge permission to reproduce copyright material in this anthology, in the form of extracts taken from the following books:

Boy by Roald Dahl, copyright © Roald Dahl 1984, extract reprinted by permission of Jonathan Cape Ltd and Penguin Books Ltd; 'The Bay of Olives' from *Birds, Beasts and Relatives* by Gerald Durrell, by permission of Collins; 'The Strength of Life' from *One-Eyed Cat* by Paula Fox, reprinted by permission of J. M. Dent & Sons Ltd; 'The Glass Cupboard' from *Fairy Tales* by Terry Jones, published by Pavilion Books 1981; 'The Man Who Was a Horse' from *Long Journey Home* by Julius Lester (Longman Young Books, 1973), reproduced by permission of Penguin Books Ltd; 'The Tibetan Envoy' from *The Spring of Butterflies* by He Liyi, by permission of Collins; extract from *Island of the Blue Dolphins* by Scott O'Dell (Constable, 1961), reproduced by permission of Penguin Books Ltd; extract from *Amish Adventure* by Barbara Smucker, reprinted by permission of Irwin Publishing Inc.; extract from *The Cay* by Theodore Taylor, reprinted by permission of The Bodley Head; 'Bushfire' from *February Dragon* by Colin Thiele, reprinted by permission of Colin Thiele and Rigby Publishers Ltd; extract from *Walkabout* by James Vance Marshall (first published as *The Children*, 1959), copyright © James Vance Marshall 1959, published by Michael Joseph Ltd.

Every effort has been made to trace copyright holders. The editor and publishers would like to hear from any copyright holders not acknowledged.

If you would like more information about the environment and the work of the campaigning organization Friends of the Earth, then fill in the form below and send it to:

The Information Officer
Friends of the Earth
26–28 Underwood Street
London N1 7JQ

Please send me information about
Friends of the Earth

NAME: _____

ADDRESS: _____

_____

_____